John Baillie

A Memoir of Captain W. Thornton Bate, R.N.

Third Edition

John Baillie

A Memoir of Captain W. Thornton Bate, R.N.
Third Edition

ISBN/EAN: 9783337075897

Printed in Europe, USA, Canada, Australia, Japan

Cover: Foto ©Raphael Reischuk / pixelio.de

More available books at **www.hansebooks.com**

A MEMOIR

OF

CAPTAIN W. THORNTON BATE, R.N.

BY

THE REV. JOHN BAILLIE,

AUTHOR OF "MEMOIRS OF HEWITSON," ETC.

"Dost thou live, man; dost thou live,—or only breathe and labour?"

Third Edition,

WITH LARGE ADDITIONS.

LONDON:
JAMES NISBET AND CO., 21 BERNERS STREET.
1862.

Cheap Edition.]

EDINBURGH:
PRINTED BY BALLANTYNE AND COMPANY,
PAUL'S WORK.

TO

JOHN LABOUCHERE, ESQUIRE,

OF BROOME HALL.

MY DEAR SIR,

IT gives me great pleasure to inscribe this volume to you. You know what it is to seek to glorify God amidst the turmoil and harassments of contact with men in daily life; and you will be able to appreciate the trial and triumph of faith recorded in these pages. The last occasion on which the brave man spoke to his ship's company—two days before his death—he urged earnestly and affectionately upon them these words:—"Not slothful in business, fervent in spirit, serving the Lord." It was an epitome of his own brief but not inglorious life. And, now that he has left us, does not he seem, each moment, to whisper down into our ear—

> "Watch, watch the hour-glass of Time with the eyes
> of an heir of Immortality!"

May we have grace to follow him as he followed Christ—manfully and meekly fighting out life's great battle, and looking for "that day" when each overcomer shall have his crown! Believe me,

Most truly yours,

THE AUTHOR.

" In the pettiness of life, note thou seeds of grandeur."

PREFATORY NOTE TO FIRST EDITION.

THE object of this MEMOIR is to shew, by a living example, how a man may combine first-rate attainments in his calling with the brightest graces of the Christian life. Hedley Vicars and Havelock were not less brave soldiers because they were not ashamed to confess Christ. And it will be seen in these pages, how a SAILOR may unite to professional capacity and to personal valour, the meek and devoted service of a disciple of the Cross. To young men especially the book is commended, in the hope that it may stimulate some lagging steps and encourage some fainting hearts.

The engravings (except the last) are from originals sketched by Captain Bate. The portrait is from a photograph taken just previous to his last departure from England.

Any profits arising from the present edition will be given to aid the Mission-work in China and in Japan.

BROOK STREET, LONDON,
December 10, 1858.

PREFATORY NOTE TO THIRD EDITION.

SINCE the publication of the previous editions, the author has received from Australia a packet of letters addressed at intervals by Captain Bate to an old Messmate, who, after serving as his first lieutenant, settled in that colony. These letters (along with some others also since received, including several to Captain Collinson, R.N.) are printed in the present edition; thus adding about fifty pages to the matter previously printed.

LONDON, 1862.

CONTENTS.

CHAPTER III.

CHAPTER IV.

CHAPTER V.

CHAPTER VI.

CHAPTER VII.

CHAPTER VIII.

CHAPTER IX.

CHAPTER X.

CHAPTER XI.

CHAPTER XII.

CHAPTER XIII.

CHAPTER XIV.

CHAPTER XV.

CHAPTER XVI.

CHAPTER XVII.

CHAPTER XVIII.

CHAPTER XIX.

CHAPTER XX.

CHAPTER XXI.

In Memoriam.

LIST OF PLATES.

MEMOIR.

> "There is a light around his brow,
> A holiness in those calm eyes,
> Which tell, though earth may claim it now,
> His spirit's home is in the skies."

"He was one of those glorious men whom one so seldom meets—of rare mental powers, a fine commanding person and manly face, at the same time with a benevolence, almost sweetness, of expression, that to see him was to yearn to known him, and to know him was to love him. The bishop read the funeral-service; the volleys were fired over the grave, and we looked for the last time into the narrow home of the mortal remains of the gallant fellow who, four days before, had been on board my ship full of health and vigour. Many a rough hand dashed away a tear on the day that the beloved Captain Bate was taken to his last home."

So wrote the commanding officer of her Majesty's ship Surprise, on the fourth day of January 1858, announcing to England the "irreparable loss" which she had sustained in the sudden removal of one of the bravest of her sons.

"Not lost, but gone before,"

he beckons other wayfarers to tread courageously in his footprints. It is the purpose of this Memoir to trace those footprints, and to stimulate the timid traveller to loftier aspirations, to braver resolves, to a calmer and more divine repose.

Lord Bacon has remarked, that "the winning of honour is but the revealing of a man's virtue and worth, without disadvantage." If ever the maxim was verified, it was in the lamented officer whose sudden removal—too early for his country, though not too early for himself—has penetrated with a thrill of grief so many hearts. "How can ye believe," said CHRIST, "which receive honour one of another?" That, indeed, was honour with "disadvantage." But those big tear-drops, wiped away by the rough hands of the British sailors that day, as they laid their beloved Commander to his rest in the foreigners' cemetery at Hong-Kong, "revealed, without disadvantage," a virtue and a worth which who would willingly let die?

CHAPTER I.

> "His eye is quick to observe, his memory storeth in secret,
> His ear is greedy of knowledge, and his mind is plastic as soft wax."

It was a beautiful summer morning in the great Atlantic, when a tight little craft was sweeping, full sail, along the shore of the island of Ascension. On board was a young "mid" whose heart beat high in the hope of a right joyous welcome; for his father was Governor of the island, and "Billy" loved and was loved with a very peculiar affection. As they "hove to" before the port, the flags in the harbour were observed to be "half-mast." The day previous, the Governor had been carried off by a fever; and the heart-stricken Middy was only in time to follow his father's corpse to the grave. Poor, dear boy! how he wept that evening, as in a quiet shady spot he cast the farewell look on the remains of his chief earthly stay! That event had an import which by and by we shall comprehend.

"Nature," says Bacon, "is often hidden, sometimes overcome, seldom extinguished." One or two glimpses will reveal to us the early bent of the subject of our Memoir.

It is told of Havelock, that, when about seven years of age, he climbed a tree one day to get at a bird's nest, and that, just as he had grasped it, the branch which bore him snapped, and down he came, nest and all, with a crash to the ground. "Were you not frightened," inquired some one afterwards, "when you found yourself tumbling through the branches?" No," said he; "I had enough to do to think of the eggs; for I thought they would be sure to be smashed to pieces." And who that knows the calm fearlessness of the hero of Lucknow can fail to detect in the little incident that which pointed to a future?

At the age of five, Willie Bate would climb some tree, and, perched on a high branch, would gaze all around, as if he would gaze out his very soul. One day, his nurse caught him in this position, and rated him rather sharply. "Oh!" replied the urchin, gravely, "I was only taking a survey." Let us carry with us this incident, and interpret in its light his future.

A year or two later, a favourite amusement was a cannon of somewhat formidable dimensions. Twice over, he burnt his eyebrows with it! and not a little was he aggrieved when at length, one day, he was seriously threatened with the withdrawal of the dangerous plaything. "What!" said he, putting himself into an attitude of importance, "I was making experiments." This incident, also, we shall find, was not without its future significance.

In his eighth year, Billy was visited with that sorest of all calamities—the loss of a wise and loving mother.

Soon afterwards, he was sent to a boarding-school, from which he would return once or twice a-year to meet his little sisters. It was in the days of tedious coach-journeys; and on the way was a dreary heath, which boyish fancies peopled with "footpads" and other terrors. Billy, however, knew no fear. In setting out, it was noticed that he invariably took with him that same favourite cannon. "If the footpads," he would say, "attack the coach *I* travel by, I am determined to have a pop at them."

Like most other boys, he was fain to live "without God." At breakfast, one morning, the family-devotion was lengthened out a few minutes beyond the allotted time. "Make haste," he was heard whispering, rather restively, "and be done with that prayer; or my egg will be quite cold."

In his thirteenth year he was transferred from school to the Royal Naval College at Portsmouth, attended at that time by some sixty or seventy naval cadets. "During his two years' residence there," says an intimate friend, "he was always among the foremost in all active boys' sports, and in practical jokes played off upon the dockyard shipwrights or other mechanics, such as putting slip-knots upon the stages which they had erected to work from, throwing their tools into the docks, painting parts of a ship white which were intended to be black; and, as these sometimes passed the limit at which jokes terminate and 'no jokes' commence, he was frequently in scrapes, and was even deemed by some a pickle." And another surviving friend writes:—"Whatever he undertook, he threw his whole heart into it—he was a whole man to it for the time: it is not to be wondered at, therefore, that, with his energy of character, he should have been a leader in fun and in mischief; indeed he was more than once on the point of being expelled."

Strange scenes were enacted in those days within that same college. The future middies were in the charge of a very ancient captain in the navy, and of a most motley group of old superannuated lieutenants and serjeants of marines, whose only discipline was the rod, and whose stern voice was almost the only sound which greeted the lads outside the class-rooms. "Commit not," says one,—

> "Thy son to an hireling, nor wrench the young heart's fibres:
> In his helplessness leave him not alone, a stranger among strange children,
> Where affection longeth for thy love, counting the dreary hours;
> Where religion is made a terror, and innocence weepeth unheard;
> Where oppression grindeth without remedy, and cruelty delighteth in smiting."

But such, alas! was the doom of the inmates of the Naval College; and deeply did Willie's sensitive heart feel the sore discipline.

Yet the young collegian owed to those two years the first steady grasp which his mind had yet taken of life's real business. It has been objected that collegians are never so good sailors as those who have gone direct to sea. Bate always looked back upon that brief season as the period when the cultivation of his taste for drawing, as well as other studies, led him to adopt that difficult and honourable branch of his profession to which he dedicated with so distinguished success the chief years of his life. "He was a high example," says an eminent naval officer, who has survived him (Captain E. G. Fishbourne, R.N.), "of what a boy might become, who spent the first two years of his apprenticeship at a college; we do not know that another system could have produced any higher."

His first home afloat was the Isis, the flag-ship of Rear-Admiral Warren; and his destination was the coast of Africa and the Cape. "I have this day," wrote the captain to William's father from Sierra Leone, "received your son on board from the Forester: he appears to be a nice, honest, John-Bull-looking fellow: very much like yourself, but better looking. You may be assured of my care of him on his father's account." Even during the brief voyage out in the Forester, so favourable was the captain's impression of him, that he offered to take him at any time, and gave his father "an elegant brace of pistols, worth ten guineas, to present to him when he was made Lieutenant."

Five years the young "mid" spent on that station, his generous, frank, unselfish temperament marking "Billy Bate" out as the general favourite, first in the Isis, then in the Thalia, and latterly in the Trinculo and in the Pelican.

A brave fearless boy, he oftentimes faced dangers, before which less resolute spirits would have quailed. "Perhaps there is no place in the world," writes an eye-witness, "where the 'rollers,' or breakers, are so grand and imposing, as at the island of Ascension. During the time they last, it is most dangerous to venture on the sea in a boat; and vessels are often in the bay for days together without being able, except by signal, to communicate with the shore. I well remember, that one day, when the rollers were unusually high, we observed a boat coming from the Admiral's ship, and making for the land. Who could be the daring adventurer, thus to tempt the perils of the deep? A glass was instantly in request; and, with no little anxiety, we watched the progress of the boat, tossed by the foaming, raging waves, as they threatened each moment to overwhelm her. Happily she reached the shore in safety; and who should be the first to land but our joyous young friend, William Bate, who knew no fear, and had succeeded in getting a few volunteers to join him in his perilous voyage? Though his father," adds our informant, "upbraided that rash risk he had run, I am sure he secretly admired the courageous spirit of his brave and dauntless boy, who seemed thoroughly to have enjoyed his hazardous adventure."

His fearless heart was as generous as it was brave. "There are few," it has been said,

> "Who deserve to have thy confidence;
> Yet weep not, for there are some, and some such live for thee."

One day, the frigate was cruising in the Bight of Benin; and, as she swept along at eight knots an hour, suddenly a shout was heard, "A man overboard!" The place was known to be infested by sharks; and, just before, some had been seen prowling about the ship. A paleness gathered on some faces, as the man was seen struggling in the waves; but one bold spirit did not shrink. A few moments, and Bate was in the waves at his side —seized the drowning man—and succeeded in keeping him above water until the boat reached them, when both, nearly exhausted, were rescued.

Even on the most trifling little occasions of everyday life, the kindliness of his generous soul would shew itself. "As his father was Governor," says the same eye-witness, "his occasional visits to the island gave William a famous opportunity of shewing attention to his messmates whenever the vessel came into harbour. At those times his friends were never forgotten; he was invariably accompanied by some of them on shore; and those left on board were always supplied with a host of good things. Frequently, very frequently, he has come to our house with a cargo of nice stores for his friends, such as jars of preserved ginger, foreign fruits, and other dainties, which he had obtained for them from his indulgent parent. One morning, in particular, I remember him coming to us in ecstasies, exclaiming, 'All right! my father has at last granted my request.' It was a fat young pig for the midshipmen's mess. 'But where will you keep him?' we enquired. 'Oh! piggy,' he replied, with a hearty laugh, 'we'll stow him away as a pet in a middy's chest, till we require him for the table.'"

One of his adventures at this period was remembered as "The Fishing Excursion." It was a birthday or some gala-day, when he had obtained for a few of his choice friends a holiday on shore. Early in the morning, they started in a boat for "a group of rocks round the point," where the rock-cod and black fish abounded; and, once there, they proceeded on an exploratory expedition to an unfrequented cove, a considerable distance off, which had the character of being infested with sharks. It was a strict order on board that any absent boat should quit the shore before sunset; but evening came, the flags had been hauled down, and still no tidings of the young fishermen. Fears began to be entertained for their safety, and a boat was just proceeding in search, when, as darkness closed in, the hapless middies made their appearance; and in such a plight! The boat had upset in the cove; and the youthful crew had narrowly escaped with their lives. They had returned over the rocks by the sea-shore, a long and difficult route; and, besides having lost some of their clothes, they were weary, hungry, and worn. William, minus a shoe, and a silver watch which he had got from his father, rather dreaded meeting him; but it was not in his frank and open nature to conceal his faults, and on the very next morning he hastened on shore and told him all, acknowledging with sorrow his carelessness, and asking pardon for himself and his companions.

The "silver watch" had a little history. It was the first he had ever possessed; and he had made an amusing bargain with his father, that, if he would only give it him, he should in return surrender to him "all the prize-money he might make on the coast."

Another day, we have a glimpse of the middy at his desk. The Pelican was lying off the island, and his father sent him word that a merchant-ship was on the point of sailing for England and that he must prepare his letters for home. Willie was forthwith on shore with his desk. "After shewing us," writes a friend, "a variety of his prized 'curios,' he produced sundry sheets of letter-paper, all closely written, and each sheet containing precisely the same news, word for word alike, save the names, which were left to be filled in. He then asked us to assist him in selecting the clearest and best-written letter for his Grandmother, an especial favourite. This selection being made, 'My dear Granny,' was inserted, and the letter folded and addressed with great glee; 'for,' said he, 'this way of writing saves me a world of trouble.'"

That day, as he sat at his desk showing his "curios," one in particular seemed to take his fancy exceedingly. It was a little box, highly polished, having the appearance of a dark reddish grained wood. "This," says our informant, "he assured us was made of 'salt-junk,' such as the sailors in days of scarcity used to get for their provisions. Hard and tough indeed it was; and we looked rather incredulously on the little box, thinking our friend wished to play some joke on us; but we afterwards ascertained that William was right, and he heartily laughed at our want of faith. The box was really made out of the salt-beef, which had been compressed, dried, and hardened, so that it bore an exact resemblance to coarse-grained wood."

But graver characteristics were already shewing themselves. "William on shore for his holidays," says the same friend, "and William on shore on duty, seemed two very different beings. Well do I remember how we used to smile at the air with which he would pass our house when in the performance of her Majesty's service, and would look round gravely and say, 'I cannot speak to-day, for I am *on duty.*'" And his father wrote:—"Willie is every inch a sailor. He is devoted to his work, and never spares any pains to make himself acquainted with his *duty.*" The characteristic was to ripen, at a future day, into the grand feature of his life.

It was on one of these periodical visits to the island, that the heart of the young mid was stunned, as we have seen, by the sad news that his revered and beloved father had been suddenly snatched away. Fondly attached to him, and clinging to him all the more warmly that his island-home seemed like the loved domestic hearth of Old England translated to the solitudes of the mighty ocean, he was anticipating, that morning, in high spirits, the old familiar welcome,—when, alas! the orphaned boy stood weeping, before night, at the side of his father's grave. "The blow," says a surviving friend, "left on his affectionate heart a deep but solemn impression, which may be considered the turning point in his career."

"Hush! e'en now, thy FATHER, speaking, answers from the heavenly land,
Tells thee how this deep affliction has proceeded from His hand.
Fear no more, for He is with thee; check each murmur, and be still;
He shall shew thee how to suffer, how to do, His righteous will."

Yes, dear boy! ANOTHER Father has taken thee by the hand now.

CHAPTER II.

"A soul redeem'd demands a life of praise;
Hence the complexion of his future days."

LADY HUNTINGDON, one evening, was on her way to a brilliant assembly, when suddenly there darted into her soul this word (committed to memory, years before, in learning the Westminster Shorter Catechism)—"Man's chief end is to glorify God, and to enjoy Him for ever." From that hour, her whole life revolved round a new centre. The guilty, trembling sinner—hitherto occupied with her poor self—gazed on the face of Him who had died for her; and as she gazed, her conscience found peace, and her heart a satisfying rest. Her whole future life became one "living sacrifice."

Into the future of William Bate the same main-spring was now imported. Before, he had won all hearts by his warm, affectionate, open, manly bearing; but now a new radiance was to be shed over all, at once within and around him. "Love," it has been said, "love to the Lord, alone is life;" that love was now to brighten a path which had little else to light it up.

Not many weeks after his father's death, the young cadet arrived in England. Transferred to the Britannia, he had found in one of his messmates just such a help as he at that crisis needed. Henry Martyn, at a similar stage of his inner life, met at Cambridge a friend who "attempted to persuade him that he ought to attend to reading, not for the praise of men, but for the glory of God;" and, for the first time, the conviction dawned upon him that he must set out upon a new course. The same gracious Lord provided for William Bate a like friend in need. A veil rests over the details of this fellowship; but night after night, at stolen intervals, did the two cadets "speak one to another" of HIM who was becoming their all in all. And before he again sailed from England, Bate had taken his stand firmly and decisively on the Lord's side. "I see no business in life," Martyn wrote one day in his Diary, "but the work of Christ; neither do I desire any employment to all eternity but His service. I am a sinner saved by grace." The young sailor had now made a like surrender; and till the day he fell at Canton amidst the tears of all his fellows, he served loyally his heavenly King, "without fear and without reproach."

Scarcely had he passed his examination for Lieutenant, when war broke out with China; and young Bate was summoned to that field where he was to pass the remaining thirteen years of his life, and where also he was to finish his brief but bright career. On the voyage out, he had the fellowship of a young officer, who united with him in daily reading and prayer; and on reaching the Chinese waters, he was installed as mate of the Blenheim, a line-of-battle ship of 74 guns. One of the officers has recorded in his Diary this entry:—"1841, March 19. William Thornton Bate exchanged into our ship from the Melville, 74. We were rejoiced to find he was on the Lord's side; and he soon made one in our midst."

On board the Blenheim, in the fore-cockpit, was a little cabin, dark, and narrow, and out of the way, in which for eight months a small knot of gunroom-officers gathered night after night to pray together and to study the Scriptures. A subject was fixed previously for each successive evening, such as the "Trinity," the "Personality and Divinity of the Holy Ghost," the "Atonement;" and for two hours, the little band of disciples would interchange their pleasant communings. Outside the cabin-door was the ship's prison, where the oaths and ribaldry of the culprits in irons not seldom disturbed the holy converse within: but only the more thankful did it make them for that grace which had made themselves to differ; and often, often did it teach them to lift their eyes upward with a fresh intenseness of longing, and sing—

"World of spirits! bright and lovely,
Where the wearied find their rest;
Where no sin, no danger enters,
Where no cruel foes molest."

The praying company went by the name of the "blue-lights"—the sailor's version of "methodists" or "new-lights" on shore. And no small trial of their faith it cost them, to brave the sneer so often curling upon the lip as they mingled with their scoffing messmates. But "by these things men live." And by these things William Bate, like the sapling-oak which the rude blast only fixes more firmly in the soil, was growing into a man of firmer nerve and of bolder and more courageous faith.

One member of the little band had, not long before, been a notorious swearer. Scarcely an hour or half-hour passed without a volley of oaths. One morning a sailor was performing some duty, and P—— swore at him most fearfully. "My dear fellow!" whispered another officer, kindly touching him on the shoulder, and in a tone of the gentlest tenderness, "swear not at all!" The arrow went straight to the swearer's heart; and before many weeks, the swearer's cabin was the chosen place of prayer. He was the ship's "second master;" and after a year or two of a bright Christian walk, he was called—first of the little circle of confessors—to enter into the rest above. A survivor, referring to these fore-cockpit meetings, writes:—"Truly can I say, and I believe we all felt, that those seasons were among the most happy and privileged of our lives."

An occasion ere long arose, to test the certainty of his Christian faith and hope.

The Blenheim had been lying some weeks off Canton, when one morning all hands were ordered to "prepare to assault the town." Situated on a plain which is swept on two sides by the river, and having in the rear a considerable mountain called the White Cloud Mountain, the city was commanded by certain forts occupying some three or four slightly elevated hills immediately behind the town. The forts were occupied by Tartar troops, whilst the city itself with its suburbs, containing a population of a million souls, was protected by a wall twenty-five feet thick at the base. Our own troops were a mere handful; but, with the courage natural to Englishmen, the command was given to take the forts. The blue-jackets instantly landed; and, almost in the twinkling of an eye, they were scaling the heights. Bate was among the first to mount the breach; and, just as he had reached the summit, he was struck below the chin by a ball. Instantly his whole chest was covered with blood; and it was thought the wound was mortal. But the gallant fellow pushed on, pistol in hand; and the next moment his pistol was struck by another ball, which cut it in two. A lieutenant and mate of the brigade were killed; another officer lost his leg, and four other officers were wounded.

The crisis was past. The "braves" fled in precipitation. And the British force was in possession of the fort, since known as the "Blue-jackets' Height."

Now at leisure to care for his wound, Bate proceeded calmly to the surgeon, who found it was only a flesh-wound. But twice that morning he had escaped death by a hair's-breadth. He was "preserved in Christ Jesus." Years afterwards he was to fall, mortally wounded, almost on that identical spot; but, meanwhile, God had a work to do in him and by him; and until that work was done, he was immortal.

> "Go, labour on! 'tis not for nought,
> All earthly loss is heavenly gain!
> Men heed thee not! men praise thee not,
> The Master praises! what are men?"

CHAPTER III.

"Teach me, my God and King,
 In all things Thee to see;
And what I do in anything,
 To do it as for Thee."

No two things more essentially differ than an instinct and a grace. Nelson could proclaim the watchword, "England expects every man to do his duty!" Leonidas could point his heroic hand at Thermopylæ to "the eyes of all Greece;" but Havelock, after a series of victories, whose recital thrilled England's great heart after a fashion it scarcely ever before had known, could write—"Away with vainglory! Thanks to Almighty God, who gave me the victory!" Even without grace, Bate would have been an earnest, steady officer; but, in the hard and often thankless task which awaited him in coming years, he manfully faced all duty, counting it his joy to please Him who had "called him unto the fellowship of His Son." A shipmate, on his return home, wrote:—"Our dear friend Bate was quite well shortly before I left, and, thank God, growing in grace."

Before the affair of Canton, he had volunteered to Captain Collinson to be his assistant for the survey of the Chinese waters. The latter, having now obtained the command of the Plover, at once secured Bate's services. "His activity and energy," writes Captain Collinson in some notes kindly prepared by him for this Memoir, "were so conspicuous, that it was only by dint of great importunity that Sir Thomas Herbert, who had succeeded Sir F. Senhouse in the command of the Blenheim, consented to lose his services, permitting him to join my ship." And thus he entered on that special line of service in which he was to spend his remaining years, with a distinction which placed him confessedly in the very front rank of his profession,—not even Sir F. Beaufort, the eminent head of the Hydrographic department of the Navy, occupying a more distinguished place.

Writing from on board his new ship, he says, of date October 30, 1841:—"My very dear brother and sisters, I ought first of all to tell you that I have been appointed assistant to Captain Collinson, the surveyor of this expedition. It leaves me very little time; for in this hitherto unknown land all our time and attention are occupied in making ourselves acquainted with it. Your last letter was written the very day I was wounded at the taking of Canton (May 26th). The others that you speak of I have not as yet received; but, alas! we are in the most out-of-the-way place you can imagine,—hard work, and as yet no results; which makes the war so tiresome;—a disposition of continued obstinacy on the part of the Chinese, so that they will not ransom the cities, and they have now stopped all communication with this province. How it will end is known only to Him who is the Ruler of kings and princes; but may it be for the honour and glory of His own kingdom! China is now indeed open: its licentiousness and idolatry are, I trust, about to be invaded: and from what we are taught and have learned of other nations, China I trust is the next to be evangelised. What a blessing it will be, if it is so ordained and our highly-favoured country made still the instrument of so good a work! I have got a splendid commentary-Bible, in one large volume, by Henry and Scott, by which I trust the Holy Spirit will so enlighten my mind that, by looking up to Jesus my only hope, I may attain to that rest for which we all live."

He now had another brush with the "braves." His ship was selected by the admiral to conduct the fleet up the Chinese Sea, and, in the attack on Amoy, to lead it into position. The place was defended by five hundred guns; but such was the panic of the enemy, that the town was captured by the British without the loss of a single man,—some mandarins being so terror-stricken as actually to lay violent hands on themselves before the very eyes of the invaders.

"They are the happy men," it has been said, "whose natures sort with their vocations." It soon became apparent that Bate was of this class. "Here," says Collinson, referring to the commencement of surveying operations after the fall of Amoy, "he received the first and only lesson in nautical surveying which I had ever occasion to give him. Educated at the Naval College, he had of course seen a theodolite; but he was not practically acquainted with its use. We landed together at our first station; and, putting up the theodolite, I took a round of angles, he noting for me. I then put the instrument out of gear—let him level it, take a few angles, and put it in the box—he next was ordered to take up a series of stations, so as to carry out the triangulation round the bay; and, on plotting our work that night, I found at once I had obtained an efficient and trustworthy assistant."

The war, however, was not yet ended; and, wherever there was a post of danger, there the young lieutenant (promoted, 11th October 1841, for his gallantry in mounting the heights of Canton) was sure to be found. One of his adventures is narrated by Captain Collinson thus:—"On the night after the capture of Chinhai, he narrowly escaped with his life. The Plover, having taken up a position inside the stakes, the Chinese in the course of the night made an attempt to burn her. He was sent to examine a junk drifting towards us, when, on boarding her and lifting the hatches, the flames suddenly burst out. Bate, the first to enter the junk, stood for a moment alone; for the boat's crew, fearing an explosion, instantly shoved off. Their officer made a leap back again, but was precipitated into the water; and not till after a critical struggle was he recovered."

Some months later, another adventure occurred. His

ship had been despatched to the northern part of the Chusan archipelago, to examine it preparatory to the movement of the fleet. On their arrival, a party landed by two boats in a shallow creek, and had proceeded with all but the boat-keepers across a low level plain towards a small isolated hill, when, leaving the others at the foot, Bate and Collinson went to the summit to look around. "Suddenly," writes the latter, "I perceived him to run forward, at the same time drawing his sword; and I soon found he was chasing a Chinaman who with sword and shield had been ensconced on the summit, watching our proceedings. A horrid shout, however, distracted our attention from the individual; and, on looking on the plain below, we found the Chinese army drawn up in array to receive us. Nothing remained but a sharp retreat to the boats, from which we should have been cut off had it not been for the determined face which Bate, in command of the rear, maintained,—keeping them in check by a cool, well-directed fire." The next morning, twenty-five in number, they went on shore; and, in the course of forty minutes, without a single casualty, dispersed the Chinese forces, killing their leader and twenty others, capturing their military chest, and setting fire to their junks. "This success," Captain Collinson adds, "was mainly owing to the prompt manner in which Hall and Bate led their men along the plain."

That spring, he was privileged to enjoy once again the old fellowship of the Blenheim. "Bate and Giles," wrote one of the little band of Christian brothers to a fourth who by this time had returned to England, "are on board the Plover, very happy and comfortable. I spent the most of my time with them when at Ningpo on leave for ten days in December. I thought of you, and felt how sweet it was to mingle with those we hope to dwell with for ever. Often, with delight, I remember the happy evenings we spent together in this retreat of mine—an unspeakable privilege! After you left," he adds, "a great alteration took place: all were scattered; and soon I shall be left alone, dear Norman to whom I am indebted more than I can repay being promoted."

Some weeks elapsed; and another illustrative incident presented itself. It was at the assault on Chapoo. "To the Plover," writes Captain Collinson, "was assigned the office of covering the landing of the troops; and, on Sir H. Gough leaving the beach, he accepted my tender of Lieutenant Bate's services as his aide-de-camp to keep up communication with the rear. Among the outward defences of the city were several horse-shoe-shaped enclosures, whence the Chinese maintained a harassing fire. Supported by two men, Bate made a rush at one of the enclosures, and was at once involved in a hand-to-hand combat with the officer commanding it—a blue-button mandarin. In the course of the struggle, both parties fell to the ground; but Bate by his superior agility remained uppermost, and succeeded in disarming his antagonist and in making him prisoner."

A few minutes later, a fresh achievement meets us.

The troops were now at the gates of the city, but without any battering train or field-piece to force them open. The commander, "apprehensive that the Chinese might rally before any men could be brought to the front," was looking round on every side with anxiety, not knowing what to do, when suddenly Bate was seen sword in hand scaling the wall alone. The next moment, he was on the summit; the Chinese, supposing him to be the leader of a party, precipitately abandoned the post; and the brave fellow, coolly descending on the other side, opened the gates to the troops.

On the same occasion, another characteristic shewed itself. Now within the city, the troops attacked a joss-house occupied by a body of three hundred Tartars, who had fled to it as their last refuge. Driven to desperation, the Tartars resisted till the greater part of them were killed. In the conflict, the 18th Royal Irish lost their colonel and nine of their men; and at last they were so maddened, that, rushing upon the survivors and upon some prisoners whom they had taken in the assault, they were about to massacre them in cold blood, when Bate, coming up, and throwing himself betwixt them and their victims, saved the poor creatures' lives. Among the rescued was the blue-button mandarin, who had just been thirsting for his blood.

It seemed as if he bore a charmed life. On the capture of another town that summer, the naval brigade was passing securely along one of the streets, when a Tartar soldier came creeping up on all fours as if severely wounded, and got close enough to take a "pot-shot" at the officers heading the party. "Bate," says Captain Collinson, who was present, "narrowly escaped the shot."

One morning, as he lay off Nankin in temporary command of two of her Majesty's ships, a state-barge put off from the shore, bearing a flag of truce. It was an emissary from the governor, with a letter addressed to the English, and containing proposals of peace. Up to that hour, the "Brother of the Sun" had never communicated with the "outside barbarian" except through the most subordinate officials. Bate was thus the first European to receive a direct overture from a Chinese viceroy.

A few weeks later, he was honoured to navigate down the river H.M.S. Blonde with the first instalment of the Chinese ransom. From on board that ship, he wrote, October 1, 1842, thus:—"My beloved sisters, having some spare time, it cannot be better employed than in communicating a brother's most affectionate love to those who are so constantly in his memory. Knowing how much disappointed you all would be, on the Blonde's arrival in Old England, not to have a line from me, I take this opportunity in addition to the many instructions already given to J——, who will relate all particulars, and answer the numerous questions so sure to be put to him about me. I am now on board this ship, and have been for the last week, in the capacity of a Pilot, having brought her down the river from Nankin; and I am too happy to tell you that in the course of another week the whole of our force will be clear of the River. By my former letters, you will have heard of my having had the fever; but I am now, I am thankful to say, quite recovered. Indeed, our whole force have been very sickly; and it is a most providential thing that the Chinese made peace when they did, for we never should have been able to carry on the war in the state we are in at present.

"I think it probable," he adds, "that I shall remain out here two years longer. The admiral has in more than one instance shewn me a great deal of kindness, and a disposition towards me which will benefit me much. It is only for you, my dears, that I live; and for this alone I am glad to give you any tidings of myself which I think may make you all happy; and, if I can only in a slight degree contribute to your comforts, and come anything near what that beloved one (whom alas! God has taken to Himself for a better purpose) was, it will amply satisfy me. But again I know, from your dear and interesting letters, that you *all three* look, in a few short years and perhaps hours only, through the merits of our Heavenly Brother Jesus Christ, to be brought to that everlasting habitation where comforts and all other earthly assistance are neither wanted nor sought after. Be assured that a knowledge of Jesus will in nowise unfit us, whatever be our calling, for the many duties of this life: indeed, I am thankful to say, that, the more I am permitted to know of Him, the better adapted I am for my professional duties, a conscientious and faithful discharge of which will carry all difficulties with ease and satisfaction. And then, again, what a consolation awaits you when called upon to leave this earthly scene! Instead of fearing, we ought rather to be glad, to quit so sinful for so glorious a world; where we confidently hope to meet those who have preceded us but a short time. May you be constant in communion with God and Jesus Christ your Saviour,—being dead to all the success of this world and to the reproaches of men which bring us into a snare! And let us never," he concludes, referring to the recent death of a Brother, "forget the chastisement of our Father, so kindly inflicted upon us for our ultimate good, that we may be led to our Heavenly Brother Jesus; and let us say, with thankfulness for it—'Before I was afflicted, I went astray; but now have I kept Thy word.'"

CHAPTER IV.

"With manifold instruction
The heirs of life are train'd,
Till, heaven's portals opening,
Their holy prize is gain'd.

"Oh! keep me ever learning,
Subdued beneath Thy rod;
Make me a better scholar,
But teach me *still*, my God!"

"PROSPERITY," says Bacon, "is the blessing of the Old Testament, adversity of the New, though the latter carry the greater benediction and the clearer revelation of God's favour." Bate had now cast in his lot decisively with Christ; and it seemed as if the Fatherly discipline demanded not a little cross-bearing.

The war being over, the whole fleet were looking for some signal recognition of his distinguished services. "It was well known," writes Collinson, "that Captain Kellett was on the eve of relinquishing his command, to return home; and Sir W. Parker, with a just appreciation of Bate's merits, had announced his intention to confer it upon him,—the command of such a vessel, well adapted to the purposes of the survey, being regarded as the first instalment of the reward which he had so justly earned. In this, however," adds the same officer, "we were doomed to be disappointed. Instead of the Starling, an unhandy little vessel was appropriated to the service. And with one officer besides himself, and a crew of sixteen men — with but indifferent accommodation — and scarcely protected from the heat, he encountered for three years the burning sun of a Chinese summer, and the not less trying storm and tempest of the winter months, so well known to those who have navigated the Formosa channel."

Manfully and without a murmur did he execute this task. "The vast advantage," Captain Collinson continues, "I received from his hearty co-operation can never be effaced from my memory. With implicit confidence in his judgment, I was relieved in a great measure from the harassing anxiety caused by the navigation of a craft which could be called neither boat nor vessel, as well as by the possibility of attack by pirates. Many instances of timely succour in cases of need in the course of this service crowd on my memory. I knew his eye was always on me; and, if I was prevented by bad weather from rejoining my own vessel, I felt certain that I should be picked up. One instance may suffice. We sailed from Amoy; and, the morning being fine, I left in a boat, to put in the coast-line, while the two vessels proceeded to sound the neighbourhood of the Merope shoals. Shortly after noon, one of those sudden storms occurred with rain and thick haze, not only entirely interrupting our operations, but compelling us to beach the boat. Here we remained, thoroughly drenched, without a chance of regaining the vessels, and prepared to take up our quarters on the beach for the night,—when, through the mist, at scarcely a cable's-length distance from the shore, the little schooner was seen, scanning every nook and corner, until the object of her search was found."

At length, the outline of the coast was completed, the whole seaboard from the Chusan archipelago to Hong-Kong being delineated with incredible labour on "ninety-five sheets of drawing paper." "Nothing, I believe," Collinson adds, "but a stern determination to do his duty, and a warm affection for myself, induced him to put up with the discomfort and harassing toil of these years."

Picturing the hidden life of the tried cross-bearer, a kindred spirit has written—

"Alone, alone—in the world alone,
Pacing the desert wild;
Say, who is this unacknowledged one,
With aspect calm and mild?

"Alone, alone—on the earth alone,
His heart seems far away,
In spirit-worlds, to our gaze unknown,
Where other sunbeams play.

"Alone, alone—in rough paths alone,
In pilgrim-garments now,
His eye discerneth a radiant crown,
Which soon shall deck his brow." *

* Snatches of Sacred Song. By the Author of "The Protoplast."

Over the inner trials and triumphs of faith in those years a veil rests; but a friend who met him at Amoy towards their close tells how he had gathered upon his whole bearing and converse a fresh heavenliness, as if in the solitude of his quiet cabin he had been drawn into a deepening intimacy with Him who delights in the broken and contrite spirit.

In the spring of 1846, the Plover was ordered home; and Bate, declining the command of the miserable little craft, which had been offered him by Sir T. Cochrane with the view of pursuing the survey of the coast to the south and west of the Canton river, returned, as the Plover's senior lieutenant, to England.

But it was only to suffer a new disappointment of his just hopes. "I naturally expected, on my arrival," Captain Collinson writes, "that his meritorious services during the war, combined with his indefatigable exertions subsequently, would be duly and cordially acknowledged. But I regret to say that this was not the case. Under the pretext that he was 'a surveying officer,' his claims were for a whole twelvemonth disregarded." And another officer, who held a command in the Chinese waters, writes:—"Sir George Cockburn, who had been first sea-lord of the Admiralty during the Chinese War, was requested to explain how it was that Lieutenant Bate had not been promoted equally with the first lieutenants of other ships engaged. The reply was, that it was an oversight, and that he felt that Lieutenant Bate ought to have been promoted for his conduct in scaling the walls of Chapoo. He even gave him a letter to Sir Charles Adam, then first sea-lord; and it was supported by another from Sir William Parker, who had been commander-in-chief during the war. But they were of no avail. The Admiralty never admit a mistake, and, unless at the instance of powerful political friends, never repair one, however unjust."

The neglect was very trying; but he had learned to "possess his soul in patience." Amidst man's coldness, a voice from his Father in heaven seemed to whisper to him—

> "Thou art praying, watching, waiting, yet it passeth not away;
> And there is not aught so sick'ning as a hope deferr'd each day:
> Grace is pledged thee, grace sufficient, for thy deepest, longest need;
> Help when thou art feeling weakness, strength for every word and deed."

The occasion was just one of those testing seasons in a man's life, when he discovers practically what his religion is worth to him. What some men on such occasions achieve by the mere force of a strong will, Bate owed to a calm repose in his God. Not sinking into a mystic quietism, but putting forth his own manly, steadfast faith; he determined to make the best of the enforced interval of rest by a course of severe professional study, contentedly waiting until He who ordereth all steps should open up his way.

Captain Collinson writes:—"Instead of languishing under the feeling that he had been unwarrantably passed over, and that the reward for the services which had made his commander a Captain and a Companion of the Bath, was not extended to him who had served as senior lieutenant throughout the same operations, he diligently set to work to avail himself of the course of instruction at the Naval College at Portsmouth."

His uniform aim was to master thoroughly whatever he took in hand; and therefore, whilst most other men would have been content with the unusual measure of attainments already reached, he who had now for five or six years been conducting operations of the most difficult nature, and with a success which had commanded the marked and almost enthusiastic approval of every party who witnessed them, was not ashamed to take his place once more in the class-room, first at Woolwich and afterwards at the College just named, during a space of nearly two years.

We have before us, as we write, no fewer than six considerable manuscript volumes, embodying the results of his studies during those years. One of them is marked, "Steam Factory at Woolwich," and relates to a variety of problems on steam navigation, illustrated by a number of neat-handed sketches. The other five were used at the College, and contain an immense number of exercises on the "Application of the Integral Calculus," on "Curvature," on "Forces," on the "Method of Indeterminate Coefficients," on the "Differential Calculus;" besides a series on "Optics," and another on "Astronomy." The general impression conveyed by a perusal of the whole is that of a singular exactness and thoroughness. He went to the bottom of everything, not content with a slip-shod, superficial idea of things, but grasping every subject with a steady hand.

There was also a warmth of affection about him, coupled with an extreme simplicity of character, which made him a perfect model of a friend and a brother. "I have now arrived safe among my dear sisters," he writes at this period to a bereaved relative, "and exchanged a life of health and activity for one of peaceful enjoyment with those from whom I have been so long separated. Alas! I wish I could have found no change amongst your own dear circle. The affliction is sore indeed to those who are left (that our family can well tell *you*); but what a glorious meeting awaits us! J—— is up to the eyes in business, all on my account, as she conceives my wardrobe not to be in first-rate order after a seven years' cruise. They all desire their kindest love."

At length, through the intervention of a friend who happened to be in a position to wield some political influence, he was promoted to the rank of Commander; and, some months later, he was selected by Sir F. Beaufort to resume the survey in the China waters. At once he proceeded overland, and took the command of the Royalist, the vessel destined for this service.

It was only to meet a fresh disappointment. The survey was one of peculiar danger, the particular coast being so perilous that it used to be said of it, "You have only to look over the side at any time, and you will be sure to see a wreck." "And yet the craft assigned to him," says a naval officer already quoted, "he found, on his arrival, to be herself little better than a wreck. She was so full of vermin, too, that she had to be sunk to rid her of them. And a crew he had to cater, as he best might, among the reckless runaways from the merchant-service."

But, nothing daunted, he once more set his face bravely to the duty laid upon him. It was *duty;* and, that settled, he meekly took up the cross, looking for the verdict of another day, when the loving Master above should pronounce the "Well done!" Meanwhile, amidst the solitudes of the coming years, he was to overhear, by the fine ear of faith, more than once or twice, the heavenly consolation—

"Toil on, toil on! Thou soon shalt find
For labour, rest; for exile, home:
Soon shalt thou hear the Bridegroom's voice,
The midnight peal, 'Behold, I come.'"

CHAPTER V.

"His love is principle, and has its root
In reason, is judicious, manly, free."

IN the way towards the eastern coast of China (it has been said) lie the fragments of a shivered continent. Great spiral peninsulas stretch southwards; and immense islands, whose interiors are unknown to us, lie about. Bordering although they do on the highway of commerce, some of them are as little known as the fanciful regions of the ancient geographers. The microcosm of a Peninsular and Oriental Steamer listens with a half-credulity to stories of flying monkeys, and prodigious serpents, and a population of cannibals, while the vessel dashes through an archipelago of islands thickly clad with tropical foliage and canopied with lofty palms. The passengers are looking towards their point of destination, and spare few thoughts to the untamed regions which lie upon their path. Yet they are skirting the precincts of a future empire, which must at some not very distant day take part in the world's history. It cannot but happen that where coal and metal are plentiful, where land is fabulously fruitful, and rain and sunshine alternate through the year, that region must be of great political and financial importance in the hands of civilised possessors. All commerce round the Cape, all communication by way of Egypt and the Red Sea, must thread the narrow channels which separate the fragments of this broken piece of earth. It has all the elements of a great future, all the possibilities of a vast empire. The age of romance is not ended whilst the islands of the Eastern Archipelago remain unexplored.

Of these islands, not the least important, from its position, is Palawan. Extending 275 miles in length, with an average breadth of 32 miles, and situated betwixt the north of Borneo and the Philippines, its coast presents to the trafficker on the great highway of commerce a series of coral reefs which, until laid down with the utmost exactness, must occasion the most serious hindrance to a safe navigation. "Each new report of the survey," Sir F. Beaufort wrote one day to Bate, "shews us how immeasurably distant from the truth our charts were." To "prosecute (as the Hydrographer expressed it) the survey of these most difficult waters," Bate was now to devote some of the best years of his life.

In the month of April (1850), he was off the north end of the island, and entered on his trying task. As the "observations" involved an incessant vigilance from his own eye, his scrupulous sense of duty kept him on one continuous stretch. The "private journal," recording his daily routine, is in this respect one of the most striking documents we have ever seen. To narrow souls which can see no glory save in the din of arms or in the smoke of battle, such labours may seem poor and inglorious; but Bate confided, for the real advancement of civilisation, less in bullets than in the removal of all barriers to mutual confidence and intercourse; and therefore he did not grudge the toil and harassments of these years.

One day, after "beating up through the channel formed by the north-east side of Palawan and the islands fronting it," he landed on "a small coral reef, ten feet high," to obtain a bearing; and, at night, on one of the small islands, he bivouacked "under a blanket on the beach." Whilst on the reef, he observed "within pistol-shot" several whales, "both common and sperm;" as many as twenty being counted in one day. On shore, the island was "thickly wooded, and without much jungle;" and, in the course of a little stroll, they came upon some hogs, besides observing, in the distance, as darkness came on, "several small fires."

Another day they "hove to and communicated with a little place called Santa Monica," where they found "about five-and-twenty houses, built upon piles, after the Malay fashion, and containing a population of forty or fifty souls." Entering a building "situated on a mound which made a conspicuous mark on the coast line," they were astonished to observe at one extremity "a figure of the Virgin Mary." The people were "a sort of half-caste Manilla, nominally under the Spanish flag, and paying annually to that government one dollar per man." Some pigs, fowls, and cocoa-nuts were met with; but the natives "shewed little desire to part with them."

Some days later, in communicating with the shore, the vessel "passed from twenty to fourteen fathoms;" and, "on heaving to, the next cast was ten," whilst, "close in shore of that, the gig struck upon one fathom." The same day, the cutter had traversed the coast a considerable distance southward, and had found the shore "fronted with coral reefs." The next afternoon, in running for an anchorage, the vessel "grounded on a reef, but bumped over it without holding." And, a day or two afterwards, the depth suddenly varied from one hundred and fifty fathoms to twenty, and then to nine; "this great and sudden change occurring within a distance of two or three cables, and when the vessel had little more than steerage-way." "What a stupendous wall," he adds,—"upwards of six hundred feet high!" The distance of this spot from the nearest shore was "only three and a half miles."

Not unfrequently, "at points where from the numerous reefs it would have been exceedingly hazardous to venture in the ship," they organised little expeditions, "with the pinnace and gig, and a week or two's provisions;" and on these occasions they encountered often the most harassing labours in "climbing to the summits of hills for the purpose of observations." In one of his official letters, he alludes incidentally to such occasions thus:—"I forward a box containing two mountain-barometers, which have received damage from the difficult ascents to some of the mountains up which they were taken."

At various distances, averaging about fifteen miles, along the coast, they found "small settlements, with a population each of some hundred and fifty souls, speaking a Spanish patois, and acknowledging allegiance to that flag." They generally had selected a site "commanding the immediately neighbouring land and enclosed in a kind of rude stockade." A small portion of the ground was cleared, upon which they grew rice, sweet potatoes, and tobacco,—but little more than sufficed for their own consumption. The people were employed in collecting tortoise shells, bees' wax, and trapang. A slight traffic was carried on with the contiguous settlements by means of canoes, in the bows of which a brass swivel or three-pound gun was generally to be seen, to protect them from the Moroos, a piratical tribe that made occasional incursions from the southward in large bodies. "I imagine," he writes, "that they are Bornean pirates, who carry on a systematic course of plunder here as elsewhere; for wherever we have been, the people have invariably expressed themselves as continually labouring under anxiety from them."

The houses were constructed of wood, and built upon piles raised eight or ten feet from the ground. In the rainy season they spoke of being visited by a sickness somewhat resembling the cholera or black vomit. They had no medical man; and on the question being put to the person administering the Government at Taiti

A Native of Palawan

how he managed when taken ill, he carelessly replied, "Oh! God is my doctor."

Proceeding southward, they found the Spanish element gradually disappear, until they came upon a population of pure Malay. "They are remarkably plain," he says; "and their expression of countenance betokens a complete absence of intellectual endowments. They make themselves, if possible, more hideous by the constant application of the betel-nut. The hair is long, and jet black; the men allowing it to fall over their shoulders and back—which gives them a shocking appearance—and the women gathering it all into a knot at the back of the head. The men's clothing consists merely of the chawat; but the person who styled himself the chief had on a Spanish shirt in addition. The women's attire is a coloured cotton garment, passed tightly round the waist and reaching to the knees. Whilst some of the women are in figure most perfect, others again present an unsightly spectacle, arising from a scorbutic affection which prevails greatly, and disfigures the whole frame. Stock," he adds, "is plentiful, the people evidencing every desire to give what little they possessed, each woman who visited the ship bringing a fowl in her arms for a present."

Bate had a singular tact in managing men, his ruling maxim being to treat even the rudest and humblest with a respectful, considerate kindness. One day, a boat's company was "in-shore" surveying, whilst the ship was doing some work further off. As they pulled along the coast, a party of armed natives was observed on the beach. Directing their course close to the shore, they displayed an English red ensign, which, from its colour, the natives interpreted into a symbol of determined hostility. A very reserved communication, however, was effected, but sufficient to discover the source of the mistake. At once the visitors yielded to their prejudices, and substituted always afterwards for the obnoxious red a white ensign. "This," says he, "won their confidence; and a most friendly intercourse ensued."

A visit was paid, one morning, to the Datoo or Malay chief. His house lay about a mile in-shore, and was approached by a pathway cut through a thick jungle and crossed at several points by a meandering stream of clear fresh water. "Emerging from the jungle," he writes, "we opened into an extensive cultivated plain, upon which were growing rice, Indian corn, water-melons, yams, and a variety of fruits and vegetables,—in full realisation of what we had hitherto only been able to obtain glimpses of through our telescopes. The Datoo's dwelling was a complete specimen of the residence of a Malay chief. It was filled with warlike weapons of every description, even a Tower flint-lock musket. He and his people, who number upwards of five thousand, are all Mohammedans."

He found also a few of the aborigines, who were living on terms of amity with the people, some of them even being in the service of the Datoo. The tribe were at some distance in the mountains, in a state of nudity, subsisting on hogs or whatever they could find, and not molesting in any way their neighbours below. The specimens he saw were "short and thick-set, having an oval form of face but sharp features, and in colour approaching the negro." They worshipped "a plurality of gods." Their weapons were the "blow-pipe," through which they "project, by condensing their breath, small poisoned arrows;" and also the spear, and the kris; and they were seldom to be seen unaccompanied by either the one or the other.

The general aspect of the country, he describes thus:—"The whole island of Palawan is excessively mountainous, the peaks attaining an elevation of several thousand feet, and some of them disposed very capriciously. Advancing northward, again, along a straight line of coast in some parts and deep bays in others, the land assumed a different look. The high mountain-ranges, instead of sending their ridges and spires close down to the sea, were generally fronted by extensive tracts of low alluvial land; and the numerous light-green patches, stretching away up the hills, and the park-like scenery which bounded their bases, bore testimony to the fact of our being in a very populous district."

One afternoon on shore, "the peaks evidencing no symptoms of shewing out," the surveying party prepared to bivouac for the night. They "rigged a small hurricane-house—lighted a large pile of wood—drew up the boat—and made all snug; then, supper over and a few songs sung round the 'blazing hearth,' things gradually subsided, and midnight found them all asleep except the man on the look-out." At one A.M. they were roused by a blast of wind and rain from the north. "I had to 'bout ship,'" he writes, "with my hurricane-house; and the men found good shelter by stowing the canoe bottom uppermost. It rained till daylight; and, in our altered circumstances, we slept till sunrise, when, just as it cleared off, the peaks all shewed out quite plain, and, by eight o'clock, the necessary observations for determining the position of the island and carrying on the triangulation (or connexion) to the south-westward were obtained." And he adds:—"At two P.M. I left the island, having first erected a station-pole, and attached a bottle to the base of it, in which a paper was placed, bearing the following notification:—'H.M.S. Royalist, Commander W. T. Bate, Royal Navy, visited the Island in the gig, and slept here on the night of the 15th July 1850, and left July 16, having obtained observations. All with thanks to a gracious and good Providence. W. T. B.'"

Seldom a week passed without some marked mercy from HIM who holds in His hand the winds and waves. "When off a small inlet," he writes, recording one of those interpositions, "we observed to sea-ward a strong rippling which approached the ship rapidly, the wind being light at the time. It came at right angles to the shore, and would have swept the vessel into a critical position; but providentially at this juncture a three-knot breeze sprang up, which enabled the vessel to 'hold her own' until the strength of it had passed. The vessel," he adds, "was within its influence about

ten minutes; and its progressive rate may be estimated at three to four miles an hour. It impinged upon the shore, in a manner similar in effect to that of a wave caused by a paddle-steamer."

Another day, when on their way to Labuan, they were within two miles of its northern extremity, steering for an anchorage at five knots an hour, when suddenly the vessel "struck upon a rock not laid down in any chart." It was low water at the time, and "the ship's keel gave two bumps, and she passed clear."

It was after a brief sojourn that autumn at Singapore, and when on his way back to Palawan "to examine and fix the positions of the various shoals fringing that highway for all vessels adopting the eastern passage to China, when late in the north-east monsoon," that an incident occurred which illustrated most strikingly at once God's preserving care of him, and his own able seamanship.

At dusk, one evening, as a heavy squall was about to burst upon them, they were making all speed to get hold of the land, and were already drawing over to the Balaban shore, when suddenly breakers were reported ahead, and the ship struck upon a coral reef. She passed easily half her length over it, but fixed amidships. The position was very critical. The night was now intensely dark, and a swell was setting in from the north-west; and the vessel bumped slightly. By and by the tide left her perfectly quiet, though her inclination was considerable; but, at two in the morning, she became "quite lively," at times receiving some severe shocks. After an unsuccessful attempt to heave her off, "she continued to thump violently during the remainder of the night, occasionally unshipping and reshipping the rudder."

As day broke, the tide commenced falling, and the vessel bumped less violently,—when, rather suddenly, she "fell over to port, having four feet under the bow, and eleven feet astern." All hands were now employed to lighten her, "one party discharging ballast and depositing it very cleverly clear of the vessel's bows by means of a shoot rigged from the forecastle, and which received the name of the 'patent railroad;' others constructing a raft of all the available spars for the purpose of receiving the wet provisions and other heavy articles; whilst the remainder were variously employed in starting water and clearing holds."

It was now low water, and the vessel had five feet under her bow, and seven astern, having been relieved to the extent of some five-and-twenty tons. As evening came on and the tide again rose, she "gave some terrific bumps;" and the "stream anchor and chain was kept at a fair strain, in order to start her, as the swell came in, from the bed of broken coral which she had made for herself." At one in the morning it was high water, and "the chain was hove upon to move her," but without success. At last, after two violent shocks, she began to "rise and fall with the swell without touching the ground;" and, in another quarter of an hour, she was riding in four fathoms, secured head and stern. The next forenoon they picked up twelve feet of her main keel,—"the only damage sustained in the misadventure."

Alluding to this scene, Captain Collinson writes:—"On one of the numerous coral reefs the vessel was nearly lost, being saved solely by the admirable manner in which her commander constructed a raft."

A few weeks afterwards, Bate was at Hong-Kong for repairs, and met his friend in the Enterprise, on his way to the Arctic Seas. "I had the pleasure on that occasion," Captain Collinson adds, "of spending six weeks with him. We sailed for Behring's Straits on the 1st of April, and he accompanied me outside the harbour some distance. A few days afterwards, happening to look up, I found something written on the beam overhead in the cabin. On examination, I deciphered it thus—'Numb. vi. 24–26; April 1st, 1851. W. T. B.' (The words are—'The Lord bless thee, and keep thee! The Lord make His face shine upon thee, and be gracious unto thee! The Lord lift up His countenance upon thee, and give thee peace!') I need not say that the inscription remained intact. And, four years afterwards, I had the gratification of shewing it to him at Sheerness, and of telling him that his prayer had been heard."

This incident, trifling in itself, is pregnant with meaning. The lonely nights on those lonely shores had been brightened by the lamp of God. Another day will declare how, as he searched the Scriptures, and "thought upon HIS name," the Lord registered in His "book of remembrance" many a memorial of his heavenly aspirations. And this it was, moreover, which made him so calm and self-possessed in every emergency: he feared his God, and he had no other fear.

CHAPTER VI.

> "Here unmolested, through whatever sign
> The sun proceeds, I wander. Neither mist,
> Nor sultry sky, . . checking me;
> Nor stranger intermeddling with my joy."

IN the course of the month of April, the Royalist was again at Palawan.

One day, as they sailed along its western coast, a white flag was observed upon the beach, and shortly afterwards a canoe, with a similar banner, paddling off towards them. On reaching the ship, the visitors "went up her side;" and great was their amazement at the "moving island," which at first sight they had taken her for. Bate welcomed them, as he always did, with kindness; though it was not easy at first to disabuse their minds of a certain suspicion of hostility which had been excited by the "clothes" on the strangers' bodies, it being the custom of the natives in a time of war to cover their nakedness with "a coat of mail." One of the men had his head completely shorn; and the other had long black hair, with a handkerchief bound round the head. Their dress consisted of trowsers and jacket, very similar in cut to the Chinese, but not quite so loose ; and the material was canvas and jean, instead of the common blue cotton of China." Firmness rather than benevolence was developed in the structure of their heads; and their eyes were exceedingly wide apart, causing an apparent hollow in the temples. The "facial angle" was acute, the features sharp, and the mouth very large, with "an unenviable row of teeth stained with betel-root."

Another day, they came in sight of a mountain 13,000 feet high, the summit quite barren, and the rocks of a columnar form, one or two rising above the general range in large pinnacles. The prevailing feature of the coast was that of broken ranges of hills, varying in moderate height, and fronted here and there by sand-bays and rocky projections. Several birds were observed flying about the ship; and a species of swallow flew on board, apparently quite tame. A vulture, too, which had accompanied the ship for some four-and-twenty hours, perched upon the maintop-gallant-yard with a sea-snake in its claws, and let it fall upon deck, but soon returned with a second, which it also let go, though not until it had very much mutilated it, every bone being separated and its head perforated.

A morning or two later, they visited a village, lying "in the bottom of a bay," and recognisable by "a large building with a red roof, and a church-spire rising from its south gable." The population numbered about five hundred; and the place abounded with pigs and fowls, besides several buffaloes. On the margin of the beach stood "an old redoubt;" and the church appeared to have been originally a fortress, having at its extremity a very old castellated tower. The land was very fertile, and afforded great facility for irrigation; but they did not seem to get from it more than a single crop in the year.

On another occasion, he set out in the gig, "to complete the southern faces of some of the outer islands." "The formation of the group," he writes, "is limestone, rising quite perpendicularly from the sea, and terminating in very sharp pinnacles. The sides of the cliffs assume various colours; and, with the number of caves and deep recesses occurring throughout, together with the beautiful foliage shooting out in every direction, the whole forms one of the most magnificent sights I have ever seen in Nature; some of the cliffs, undermined by the sea to an extent of fifteen or twenty feet, impending to an alarming degree when viewed from a position immediately underneath them. Among the various birds seen hovering about them, is one resembling a swallow, whose nest is so eagerly sought after, that it forms an extensive article of traffic throughout the eastern archipelago. The natives move about in very small canoes to collect it. They go under one of these impending cliffs, and with marvellous dexterity ascend the face of them, crawling in and out of the crevices in search of the nest. Nearly every cliff bears traces of their assiduity in hunting for this luxury; for pieces of bamboo, with long lines attached, may be seen, everywhere, thrust into the rock for the purpose of facilitating their ascent."

Some weeks afterwards, he visited a village "very prettily situated immediately under a high precipitous limestone cliff full of caverns and crevices and interspersed with beautiful sprigs of foliage." On landing, they were met by "a square stockade, with four brass guns—one of four pounds calibre—shewing through ports about twenty feet from the ground." Immediately in the rear was a large house, the residence of the chief; and, a little further back, the "Court-house," which was furnished with "stocks, a wooden shoe, and a terrible six-tailed scourge made out of buffalo-hide," which is administered by "laying the culprit prone with his face to the ground, securing his ankles in the stocks, and then inflicting on his bare posteriors as many as twenty-five lashes." Still further to the rear was a gallery, leading to a crevice immediately under a high cliff; and, ascending a bamboo ladder, the party found themselves in "a cavern in the side of the cliff fifty or sixty feet from the ground"—a place of refuge to which the natives retreated on being surprised by an enemy. Returning to the village, they saw handlooms and spinning-wheels, on which the women were manufacturing, from materials grown on the spot, fabrics for home-use.

The miserable craft was a source of constant discomfort. "In the strength of the squalls," he writes, one day, "the vessel remains moderately steady, occasionally giving one or two heavy plunges; but, immediately the wind relaxes, she jumps and rolls about tremendously. This was the case all last night, and particularly when the wind came off the land." And, another day:—"Our sails are constantly splitting, and the roping giving way. So little are our sails to be trusted, in case we require them to extricate the ship out from difficulties which are constantly to be apprehended, that it is a perpetual occasion of anxiety to me." And, again, thus:—"At 10.30, a most violent squall burst upon us. It caught the vessel a little on her broadside, and made her careen several degrees. The night was dark; and torrents of rain fell. Whilst walking the deck, expecting every moment the cable would part, how frequently did the thought of the 'anchor' as the beautiful emblem of 'hope' occur to my mind!"

It was thus he calmly reposed day by day in his God.

"Holy teachings have been with thee, whisperings of the world to come—
Song of angels—gleams of glory—glimpses of thy heavenly home."

—And new occasions were continually arising for adoring the Lord's preserving care.

A party landed one afternoon on "Three-peaked Island," to take observations. Ascending the peaks, they found the rocks so steep and the footing so uncertain, that, "to secure the safety of their lives as well as of the instruments, he determined to have the boat's cable bent on to a palm-tree near the summit;" and, accordingly, a sailor proceeded upward with the rope, the commander immediately behind, until it was properly made fast. "I was sitting," Bate writes, "on the edge of the cliff about fifty feet in height, when suddenly the gig's crew from below called to me to 'take care;' for a heavy piece of rock, which had yielded to the man's foot who was climbing above me, was coming down by the run. With the caution, I received upon my head a violent blow which cut it open. Providentially I had on a hat (helmet-shape) of considerable thickness: otherwise, if not killed on the spot, I must have been knocked senseless over the precipice."

A month elapsed; and he writes:—"At 1 P.M. to-day, we saw Balaban peak; and glad was I to behold it. We have now wellnigh got to the end of Palawan; and we may soon look forward to receiving our letters. God's providential care has been singularly manifested towards us. We have been preserved from many dangers, seen and unseen. We have not lost one of our number, either from accident or from sickness. And our work has been attended with peculiar blessings. Everything whereunto we have put our hand has prospered; and this, not by our own wisdom, but by the grace of Him who has said, 'Commit thy works to the Lord, and thy thoughts shall be established.'"

And, a week or two later, he adds:—"It was this day two years that I embarked on board the Peninsular and Oriental steamer Ripon (Captain Moresby) at Southampton for Hong-Kong, in order to take up my present command. The time has passed rapidly; and many incidents, which will ever be fresh in my recollection, have occurred in the period. My public duties, I trust, have been discharged in a manner satisfactory to those who entrusted me with the execution of them. I wish I could say the same of my duties to my Heavenly King. I am not conscious of ever giving satisfaction; for, even if I had done all, I should still be an unprofitable servant."

CHAPTER VII.

> "With all its caves,
> Its hollow glens, its thickets, and its plains,
> Unvisited by man."

It is a touching thought which a living writer has uttered—

> "Hark! what is that voice I hear?
> Whose can be that prayer,
> Daily sounding in mine ear,
> Give me to drink?
>
> "May I ever recognise
> Thee, in Thine, before mine eyes,
> When their destitution cries,
> Give me to drink!
>
> "May each suppliant at my door,
> Shelterless, unclothed, or poor,
> Vainly urge that prayer no more,
> Give me to drink!"

Bate's daily life was that thought translated into action. In the spring of 1852, as the Royalist lay off Hong-Kong undergoing repairs, the small-pox broke out on board, to the great consternation of the ship's company. The first seized was the clerk; and, to prevent the infection spreading amongst the crew, the captain actually had him removed into his own cabin! He had scarcely recovered, when Bate himself caught the disease, and desired to be taken on shore to hospital. "The men," says an eye-witness, "were most of them in tears, as our beloved commander was put into the boat; for he had every appearance of having it severely."

To an old messmate he thus describes the attack:—"During the early stage, I became frequently more or less delirious. My symptoms were very severe—the pox approaching a confluent form; but, thank God! the protective power of the vaccination, which I had received when an infant, operated most powerfully, and mitigated the disease at the most dangerous period. I took it almost immediately after Cave got well, and, I think, the day he left my cabin. It is a fearful disease. I had no conception of its malignity. The pustules even appeared in my eyes, and under the hard skin of the soles of my feet, which was most painful. However, I do indeed thank God for the visitation, and would not have had it otherwise for worlds. It has done me a great deal of spiritual good, I hope; and I do trust the sickness will be sanctified to me. The kindness of my officers has been beyond all bounds; and the anxiety they evinced when I was first taken ill and ultimately was obliged to be hoisted over the side in my cot, brought forth tears which I was glad to have recourse to my bedclothes to conceal from them. I have been up now four days, but am still very weak."

A month or six weeks afterwards, he wrote to a young relative in England:—"I am sure you must have come to the conclusion that I had quite forgotten you. I have only just been mercifully raised up from a bed of sickness, having had a severe attack of small-pox. I am still very weak, and cannot write so long a letter as you deserve or as I wish. Do you remember our walks, wasps' nests, kite-flying, and all those happy little amusements? I do often; and they bring, each of them, many pleasing associations. We shall all be too old and big to enjoy them again, I fear. I hope you are all well. I hope *you* are thankful for the health you enjoy. I feel my sickness has been a great blessing to me! and I would not have been without it for worlds. I trust it has made me a better man, and led me to consider more seriously how little we are profited if we gain the whole world and lose our own souls; for what is there *in the world* which we would barter our souls for? Let me entreat you to 'remember *now* thy Creator in the days of thy youth,' and not to put it off, as many do, till a more convenient season. God is better pleased when *young people* dedicate themselves to Him, than He is when they only give the mutilated fragments of old age to Him. God bless you!"

As he lay on his sick-bed, he had received from a kindred spirit in England a letter which greatly comforted him. "You will see," wrote Sir Edward Parry, "that I have taken a liberty with your name which I venture to think you will excuse. Although the current of life, and its necessary business, goes so fast as to allow us little time for correspondence, we (at Haslar) beg you to believe that we ever and very often think of you with sentiments of affectionate esteem. As time goes on, and eternity is nearer at hand, we cling more closely to the 'little flock,' the 'household of faith,' the faithful followers of a crucified and risen Redeemer. May the Lord be ever with you to keep and bless you! I see, by the List, that two years and a half of the Royalist's commission have expired, so that I trust it may not be very long ere you bend your steps homeward. Lady Parry and all our Christian circle unite with me in every good wish at this blessed season." The enclosure was "a proposed Union for Prayer for the promotion of Religion in Her Majesty's Navy," and suggested "that every Sunday morning betwixt Seven and Eleven the spiritual wants of the Navy should be brought before the throne of grace, that all orders of men in the Naval Service, from the highest to the lowest, might be led to a serious concern for their souls, and for the spiritual welfare of their fellow-men; and in particular that officers might entertain a just sense of their high responsibility as regards the spiritual as well as temporal interests of those over whom they are placed, exercising a spirit of wisdom, justice, love, and a sound mind."

So to live, was Bate's own unceasing aim. On the fly-leaf of each of his Journals he had this motto:—

"And is this all? Can reason do no more,
Than bid me shun the deep, and dread the shore?

Sweet moralist! Afloat on life's rough sea,
The Christian has an art unknown to thee:
He holds no parley with unmanly fears;
Where Duty bids, he confidently steers,
Faces a thousand dangers at her call,
And, trusting in his God, surmounts them all."

And the motto was engraven on his very inmost heart. "Quiet and retiring," says Captain Collinson, "his charity was like his faith, ever working, but so silently that you came upon it by accident." His godliness was a part of himself—a thing *in* him, and not needing to be put on. We shall by and by see how legible to all the "living epistle" at length became.

Scarcely had he again reached the old scene of his labours, when an incident occurred which he used to regard as one of his most hair's-breadth escapes. One evening, some months afterwards, on revisiting the spot, a little party was pulling ashore; and Bate, recalling the incident, and turning to an officer who in the interval had joined them, said:—"The gig had been absent all the morning in the head of the bay (leaving the ship to cruise), when, on her return, she was chased by seven large prahms full of pirates, who had been hidden amongst the mangrove bushes. All the ammunition had become damp; and the only resource was to escape as quickly as possible. The prahms at last were gradually stealing on the wearied crew, and, with fierce shouts and yells, were making sure of their prey, when most opportunely the Royalist hove in sight. This caused them to put about; and they were quickly hidden amongst these islets." And he added, with a

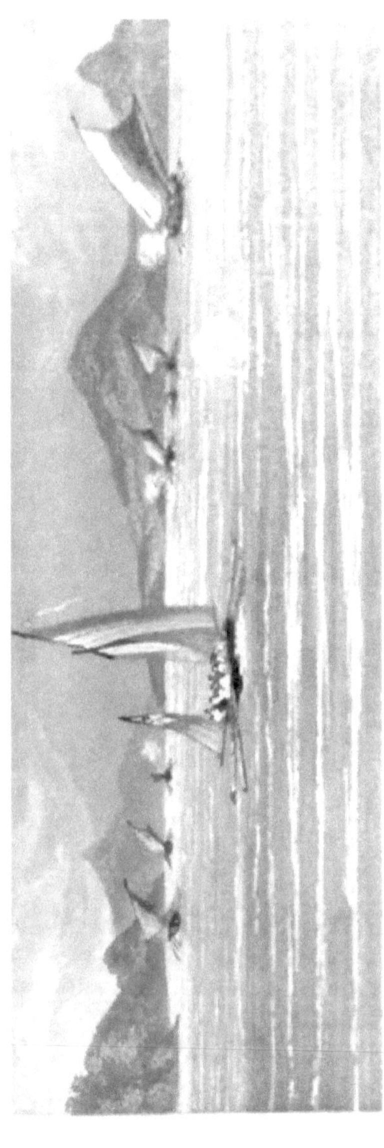

peculiar emphasis :—"Always live so, that, when death approaches, you can look him in the face: then there is nothing to fear."

A week or two later, he had an escape of another kind. It was a squally morning, and their last cast had given fifteen fathoms, when suddenly the vessel was on the edge of a shoal, the depth now seven fathoms, and "rocks distinctly visible under the bottom." Within a few cables of her lee-beam was the "light green water, and the wind and swell setting her fast towards it." Not a moment was to be lost. "Caught dead upon the weather-side of a reef," the ship "lay like a log upon the water." "Sail had to be made," he writes, "and way given to her before we could stay. There was no room to wear, and every instant the rocks under us looked nearer, the soundings also confirming it. By God's providence, we skirted the very edge of the reef without touching, and tacked. We soon deepened our water; and thankful indeed we were for this deliverance from a position eminently critical. Had we touched the ground, our case would have been hopeless, as each succeeding swell must have carried the vessel further on, if it did not break us to pieces."

On his way, he had touched at Labuan, anchoring off "Coal Point." Going on shore to examine the coal-measure, he found a large quantity of coal stacked near the jetty; it "looked very good, resembling our Newcastle," with not quite so much gas, but in other respects almost equalling it. Three hundred labourers were employed at eightpence a-day, and they had dug up 1080 tons during the last month. The Peninsular and Oriental Company had made a contract to be supplied with 400 tons monthly, the price twenty shillings per ton. "I think," he writes, "it only wants a little more energy on the part of the Eastern Archipelago Company, or its agents, to make these mines a considerable source of profit to themselves and advantageous to the island generally."

The survey was vigorously prosecuted, notwithstanding the incessant perils and harassments. "At eight o'clock," he writes, for example, one day, "the dingy was despatched to ascertain the practicability of landing, as it was my intention to sleep on shore, so as to be ready for the observations on the morrow. Soon after, we landed all our gear, amidst an incessant rain, and the sea breaking heavily. It was rather a laborious task, having to wade with our traps through water up to our waists over a very uneven coral bottom." And, after getting "some good observations," he adds:—"At 7, just as we had finished dinner and were about to make all snug for the night, the water shewed symptoms of flowing as far as our tent. At 7.30 we were obliged to take everything out and deposit them in the jungle near the fire. Frequent rain-squalls were passing over; and at last we were fairly driven into the jungle by the tide. We sat in the jungle the greater part of the night round a fire, with showers of rain occasionally to refresh us."

Cowper, in one of his odes, writes—

"Who seek a friend should come disposed
To exhibit, in full bloom disclosed,
The graces and the beauties
That form the character he seeks,
For 'tis a union that bespeaks
Reciprocated duties."

Bate had the happy art of winning the affections of all who were about him; and he did it unconsciously by his own warm, friendly sympathies. "Numerous were the kindnesses," says a shipmate, referring to this period, "which he never lost an opportunity of shewing whenever a chance occurred. Even when a man was reported to him, he gained him, by his good advice and by his own consistent walk, to acknowledge his fault; and rarely was it repeated."

Christmas was always a merry day on board; and, that year, it produced an effusion which the reader will not grudge to peruse in the full proportions of its own rough Doric:—

"SIR,—An opportunity offering, which we have all been anxiously waiting for, viz., (Christmas day)—for expressing a few of our sentiments, and deeming this the most propitious time of the year, which, in accordance with the custom of our good old ancient times, we are happy to say has been handed down from our forefathers and has fortunately not degenerated, but we trust in accordance with the rising generation, the feelings have become more susceptible of the obligations we owe for any acts of kindness shewn us, the kindly feelings and good will of our superiors have been duly appreciated by us all. It has been our lot to sail with many Captains, not one of whom is fit to be a patch on your back. The fatherly treatment we have always received from you whilst we have had the pleasure of serving under you, and which never can be equalled, will always be remembered by us all. Although many hardships, which necessarily belong to the duty we are now engaged on, must be met with,—it is greatly lessened when we see that our noble, true-hearted, and ever-respected Commander endures as much, and infinitely far greater, than those, whose humble lot it is, whose heart and soul, goes with these few lines.

"As another instance of your great goodness, which is, as each succeeding morning dawns, brings forth fresh lustre to the receding day, so is every fresh act of yours.

"The present that you have so handsomely made us, wherewith to cheer our Christmas board, is greatly appreciated by us all.

"We beg the acceptance of the following trifle [a beautiful filigree silver card-case of Chinese workmanship], as a slight token for our regard and esteem. We earnestly hope you will enjoy a merry and a happy Christmas, and a New Year when it comes. May your health be good and your happiness as great, the survey you are now employed on be soon and satisfactorily finished, speedy promotion, and a happy return to Bonny Old England, is the earnest wish of

The Ship's Company, one and all,
of
H. M. S. S. Royalist.

"Captain W. T. Bate, Esq.,
H. M. S. S. Royalist,
North-west Coast of Palawan."

CHAPTER VIII.

"I think not of to-morrow,
Its trial or its task;
But still, with child-like spirit,
For present mercies ask;
With each returning morning,
I cast old things away;
Life's journey lies before me,—
My prayer is for to-day."

"WE may judge," it has been said, "by our regard for the Sabbath, whether eternity will be forced upon us." Bate *loved* the Lord's-day. "Welcome another Sunday," he writes. "With what pleasure do I look forward to this day of rest! What a merciful provision it is! 'The Sabbath was made for man!' I trust we appreciate it; for our six days are indeed spent laboriously, and we need rest for both mind and body." And the usual record follows:—"Performed divine service on deck A.M. and P.M. The day passed off with its accustomed quietness." He loved the Lord's-day, because he loved the Lord Himself; and, without forcing his own way on others, they saw that *he* felt it 'a delight."

One day, a little party, consisting of an officer and four men, went on shore to make observations. Ascending a conical hill some three hundred feet above the level of the sea and denuded of foliage but covered with long dry grass, they suddenly found themselves pursued by a conflagration, which had been kindled by the lighting of a pipe. So rapidly did the flames spread, that the party, as a last resource, struck over the brow to the left, threw themselves into a steep gorge thickly clothed with jungle, and were carried to the base of the hill. One poor fellow was overtaken by the fire, and, after running through it till nature was exhausted, fell and rolled over the burning embers down the steep incline a distance of two hundred feet. "With the exception," Bate writes, "of a small portion of flannel, every particle of clothing was burnt off him; his feet, hands, and knees were lacerated and completely charred; nearly the whole of the epidermis was off the body; and the limbs were literally baked and quite stiff. The theodolite, which he was carrying, must have been burnt off his back; some of the strong framework was broken, and only a few charred fragments of the box were picked up. At 3.10 P.M. he was brought on board, quite naked, but in full possession of his senses. He was very restless, jumping in and out of bed, and at times suffering intense pain. He could not be induced to take medicine, but drank frequently of tea. At five he became more quiet, turned upon his right side, and, fifty minutes afterwards, died without a struggle. Poor fellow! he was taken away suddenly, thus leaving another warning for *us* to be ready."

Writing to an old brother-officer, he refers to this affecting incident again thus:—"The triangulation of Palawan comes out beautifully. Our last cruise has been very pleasant, and the time has passed away like a span. It was, however, damped by a lamentable accident, which terminated in the death of poor old Fowler. Just to the westward of Malampaya Table, there stands in prominent relief a barren conical hill, excessively steep in ascent and about two hundred feet above the water. I sent Calver to take a station on its summit. He had ascended only two-thirds of the way when the interpreter, Mr Peters, after lighting his pipe at the base of the hill, inadvertently set fire to the long grass. It spread so rapidly that it overtook Calver and his party before they had time to see where they could go to escape from it. They had no time for deliberation, and consequently performed a most desperate feat in throwing themselves over the cliff into a gorge which was thickly clothed with jungle and which providentially prevented them falling further. Poor old Fowler was carrying the theodolite, and was behind the others: the fire caught his clothes, and, as if eager for more victims, passed on, leaving its burning embers to complete his destruction. Poor fellow! he strove gallantly to the last, when, exhausted, he dropped; and a fall of upwards of ninety feet projected his body through the charred bushes on to the beach, presenting to the panic-stricken boat-keepers a spectacle too horrible to relate. The body was perfectly naked and burnt most fearfully. Fragments of the theodolite were picked up on the beach near where he fell, the box being (with the exception of one side) entirely consumed. He was brought off immediately, in great pain. He was perfectly sensible when picked up, and continued so to the last.

"Mr Peters," he continues, "on seeing the body emerge from the jungle, and knowing that he had innocently been the cause, and probably thinking the rest of the party had met a similar fate, rushed frantically up and down, and disappeared in the jungle, where we lost him for twenty-four hours. As the reports were so conflicting as to the fate of Mr P., I weighed and beat up to the spot, sending boats on ahead to search for him. We also fired guns occasionally, to apprise him of the proximity of the vessel. The next morning he was found in a most miserable plight. His own account was, that he recollected nothing from the time he saw Fowler's body until he was awoke as it were by a shower of rain in the morning, when he discovered that he had fallen over a precipice and was held in suspension by the thickness of the underwood. Fowler struggled in violent pain for two hours after he was brought on board. His cries were so great, that it was thought advisable to rig a small place for him abaft; and, very soon after being brought there, he became faint, and at last died without a pang. We made a coffin, and buried him at the base of the hill where the accident occurred. It is a snug, pretty little spot;

and I can assure you none could tell the anguish of my heart when the whole ship's company were assembled in solemn silence round the grave to pay the last offices of respect, and I for the first time had to read that beautiful introduction to our Burial Service—'I am the resurrection and the life;' and I trust we all felt on this occasion the force of that touching portion of the 90th Psalm—'In the morning it is green and groweth up, but in the evening it is cut down, dried up, and withered.' We set about making a tablet to put on the grave; but, before it was completed, at five P.M., it came on to blow from the westward, and we were obliged for the safety of the vessel to weigh. I shall (*D.V.*) put it up another time."

And he adds:—"We had an excellent opportunity of fixing the York breakers, and nearly fixed the ship on them. I think we only escaped by half a cable. I landed on the Half-moon Shoal in July, and just escaped on board in my gig when it came on to blow furiously. We were for eighteen hours hove-to under close-reefed topsails, with a sea as high, if not higher, than that which we experienced the first time we crossed the China Sea. The position of the ship was a critical one, and caused me no little anxiety."

In the intervals of the surveying operations, he used to enjoy little parleys with the natives. One day, "accompanied by the doctor, the paymaster, and young Collinson," he "visited a 'sultan.'" "The old gentleman," he writes, "although suffering from rheumatism in his legs, came out to meet me as we approached his home.

A good shake of the hand followed; and we were all soon squatted inside the *Palace*. Seeing that I wore my 'kilt' out of compliment to him, he immediately sent for the Red Coat, and habited himself with it. It had been carefully preserved, particularly the epaulettes, which were wrapped up most elaborately, first in wool, and then in no end of layers of cotton cloth. Being provided with a good interpreter, I was able to get some information about these people. They number about five thousand. The Sultan has absolute power, and inflicts the punishment of death in cases of adultery or of theft. They have no punishments for minor offences. The mortality is not great; and the principal malady appears to be dropsy, depending on disease of the heart or lungs. I saw one poor creature in a wretched state, suffering from the latter; and yet he had a large kris stuck on his sarong with all the air of a warrior. Their sickly season is generally in July and August. They sow their paddy in July, and reap in January or February; only one crop in the year. We were told that a few months since they had been visited by a fleet of pirates, who, however, had not committed any act of violence. We could not induce them to shew us their women; their excuse was, that they are 'too much frightened at the white men.' The sultan gave me an excellent specimen of a native sword and shield—his own, in fact, which he used, and which was taken from his bed-side. We returned to the ship at 5 P.M. much pleased with our trip."

On another occasion, he visited a Malay "Infant-

School." There were "some score of naked young children going through their devotional and athletic exercises." The schoolmaster was dressed in the native costume—a striped blue shirt worn outside, and a very short pair of drawers. He played the tom-tom; whilst the children finished off with the fandango. The mistress wore the sarong of the Malays. Bate was so pleased, that he asked them off to see the ship; and, next day, two canoes-full arrived, and had a grand feast composed of plates of raisins, sugar, biscuits, and tea—to them unknown luxuries. After having satisfied their curiosity on board, they amused the crew with their wild dances, wrestling, and sword-exercise, and finished the evening with singing their vesper-hymn.

During the two following years, he prosecuted his labours with an untiring energy, and oftentimes under the most harassing difficulties. "Went to bed dead-tired," he writes, for example, one evening. "The heat is very great; and it is most trying work taking up stations exposed to the sun without a breath of air." Then, at other times, he would be out "observing the stars," and not retire to rest for three or four successive nights. And, worse than all, the wretched craft was a constant vexation to him, especially if sickness shewed itself. "With the number at present on the sick-list," he says, on one occasion, "we can scarce find a dry resting-place for them; for such is the leaky state of the vessel, that the lower deck is flooded in an ordinary double-reef topsail breeze."

Meanwhile, he was growing, silently but steadily, in grace. Too actively occupied in the realities of the daily battle of life, he had no time and no heart to "gauge feelings" or to "count frames." But an occasional glimpse is given into the secret springs of his inner life. Here is one:—"Performed divine service A.M. and P.M. Preached from Ps. xxv. 7, on 'the sins of our youth.' Crew attentive, and appeared to listen with eagerness. May the Lord bless my feeble labours! Out of the most unworthy vessel He can get honour to Himself; and I am sure He could not have chosen a worse instrument. I trust we all appreciate the Sabbath. How needful the day of rest to a surveying vessel!"

Elsewhere in his journal are incidental illustrations of his firm but considerate discipline. "To-day," he writes, "I had to investigate seven charges which the first lieutenant brought against Mr Fleming, the gunner, for insubordination and violent language. He pleaded guilty to all upon my explaining their nature, and expressed much sorrow. I have given him some little time to atone for the misconduct; and, if I see it genuine, I shall overlook it. He is a quiet kind of man, but hot-tempered when put out." And another day, he says:—"I had another case of drunkenness amongst the boys brought before me this morning. I think this sin and many other offences would be less frequent than they are, if the Admiralty allowed Captains to exercise their judgment in awarding punishments for them. If judicious chastisement was allowed, sins might be eradicated before they made head; whereas now they must be fully developed, to authorise the commanding officer inflicting the only punishment left for him, namely, flogging at the gun."

Wherever he went, he left among the natives the most favourable impression of his kindness. Arriving one day at an island which he had visited the previous year, he found the "captain of the fort" exceedingly attentive and hospitable, and "very anxious to have an English flag to display at his look-out tower whenever an English ship should appear." And he adds—"There was certainly a marked difference in the people's conduct towards us this time. They appeared to have such confidence in us, and treated us as if they felt that we were really friends, and had given a substantial proof of it by liberating two of their countrymen and keeping them so long on board without making any charge. One man said, 'Oh God, how good!'"

In a letter to Mr P——, who had formerly been his first lieutenant and who had now proceeded from England to Australia and had settled there, we have some interesting glimpses into Bate's daily life during those years, as well as into his genial and warm-hearted and loving nature. "I have received both your letters," he writes, on board the Royalist, off Hong-Kong, March 1, 1853, "the first commenced on board the Chusan, and the second dated October 18, at William's Town, which came to hand a few days since. And now, old fellow, let me tell you how delighted I was to hear that you were not only married, but also in a good situation in the land where all your hopes and wishes are centred. Most sincerely do I congratulate you, my dear P——, on your happy union; and oh, what pleasure it would give me if I could only one fine morning anchor the little vessel *close* off your offices! Would not I beat you up for a breakfast, if we arrived early, although the quartern loaf is 2s. 6d. and the *three* rooms £100? We should *all* be so delighted to see you; and I know that you would 'reciprocate' (as the Yankees say). I am going to office, 9 A.M., so this is the first instalment of my letter.—*March* 7, 6.30 A.M. My Sunday routine here is—Service on board, as usual; visit the mission, afternoon; at four attend service at the Cathedral; dine with Captain Parker after (where I always meet Price and Mackay); and then we adjourn to Mr Johnson's (American missionary's) prayer-meeting.

"I must now," he proceeds, "begin to tell you something of our last cruise. From Hong-Kong we sailed on the 9th of April for Palawan direct. For the first three days, we had a strong north-easter, which made nearly all hands sick. We anchored at length off the north of Palawan, remaining a day to complete the coast-line and to get a night at the stars. I then pushed on (a boat in-shore all the time running another line of soundings) for Ooloogan Bay, from which we commenced the survey of the coast to the northwards, and which you know was passed over when we first went down. By the 1st of June, we returned to Ooloogan Bay, having finished it all. We found some beautiful anchorages amongst the islands, and it was altogether a delightful trip. As the Admiral had promised a steamer, and I had arranged that Ooloogan Bay should be the rendezvous, I buried a bottle with intelligence of our whereabouts on Observatory Head two feet north from the foot of the old tree, which still bears your initials. We then pushed on to the southward, sounding and filling up wherever it was wanted. I had two beautiful star-nights, with my little tent pitched on the southernmost rock immediately north of Long Point, where you and I once met just before returning to the ship one evening. Jogging on down the coast, we went bump upon a coral patch with our '*leading marks*' on. It was not far off Albion Head. We remained hard and fast for six hours, and then got off without damage. We had no sooner got into the Bay than the S.W. breeze came on, and brought with it that horrible swell which, you know so well, gets up after a week's calm weather. The old Sultan received me in his *red coat*, and asked for you: they were very civil, and of course abused every one except themselves for being pirates. I must now go to office. God bless you and *yours*. To be continued."

He "continues" thus:—"*8th, Night.* I dined with Mr T—— last evening, and talked a great deal about you and yours. Spartan arrived to-day; and Cleopatra sails on Thursday morning for dear old England. Kelsey and Strong go home in her. Miller and Henderson will be the next to go; and then we shall have got rid of all the old hands. They were both very good men. But I must now revert to our trip. We arrived at Labuan, and had an office at the Government place, and passed a very pleasant month. We stirred them up, and succeeded in getting a jetty built by subscription: it runs out over the flat sand-bank which extends opposite the Government offices. It is now called the 'Royalist Pier.' After leaving Labuan, we proceeded to Ooloogan Bay, having fixed the Royal Captain and Bombay shoals on our way. From Ooloogan we went direct to Malampaya Sound, and a more magnificent harbour I do not think exists. We traced the course of the pirates, and the spot where they were concealed when they first came out upon us. I have called it 'Pirates' Bay;' and a beautiful, snug little anchorage it is. I regret, however, to tell you that beside a lovely rivulet which disembogues on a sandy beach in the head of it the remains of poor Tozer lie. He died a few days after we arrived, from the effects of excessive drinking when on liberty at Labuan."

A fortnight later, he proceeds:—"*March 25th.* I have been so intensely occupied about the charts and observations, that I have not had a moment to spare. I send them off by this mail. The survey of Malampaya Sound was most delightful, and we pitched our tent on the *very summit* of Malampaya Table. It took us two days to get up; and such a scramble as we had to reach the top! We were literally walking (when on the ridge) upon the trunks of trees; and at the summit we could not get *terra firma* on which to place the theodolite. We remained up three days, in consequence of the cloudiness of the weather, but succeeded at last in getting a beautiful eye-sketch and a few good angles for the triangulation of the Sound. We were so hard up for water the first night, that I paid six dollars for a gallon to make the men some tea. We took nine hands up and all the officers who could be spared. The doctor could not come on account of the sick. The height of the mountain is about 3600 feet. We had the Governor of Oai-tai and another officer as companions, and they became most intimate afterwards, we (while the ship was lying off Panbol) going over to visit them, and they all returning it and sleeping on board. We laid quite close off the stockade, and the natives used to come in and out of the ship as if it had been their home. The children used to come on board of an evening to dance and sing. By the way, you should have seen the figure our party cut after we came down from the mountain. We never had washed or put on a clean shirt up there; and, what with the dirt mixed with blood caused by the wood-leeches and brambles, we were as filthy as we could well be. When stripped, I looked as if I had been flogged fore and aft instead of athwartships. The rest were nearly in the same plight; for we had to ascend on our bellies and descend on our bottoms,—it was so steep in some places. Young Collinson, of course, was in his glory, and grinning the whole time. Millman went nearly mad with excitement; and Jack swore it was the *highest* and most difficult place any one ever tried to get up, and made themselves out to be the most wonderful heroes when they returned. The yarns they spun on the lower deck were as ridiculous as they were exaggerated and untrue."

And, some days later, he adds:—"*March* 30. The mail sailed on Monday, and with it I despatched all my tracings. I shall be heartily glad when it is over. I have made an official application to be ordered home in the Royalist at the end of this year, as I expect the reefs will be finished. I do not think I shall ever be induced to take a surveying-ship again,—it is too much drag upon me, and leaves no time for more profitable employment. I intended this to be a very long letter. We are just off, and in such confusion! Pray for us. God bless you!"

The craft grew more and more wretched, until at last, in July 1853, he received a despatch from the Admiral anouncing the resolution of the Admiralty to suspend for the present the survey of the China Sea, and to sell the vessel or break her up. On arriving at Hong-Kong, she was found capable of making the voyage home; and, after a month's handling by "Chinese caulkers and European artificers," she was on her way with her commander and ship's company to England.

During a brief sojourn at Singapore on the way, he wrote to his former messmate some hurried lines, containing a few details, thus:—"*Jan.* 15, 1854. My beloved old P——, We have just arrived from Hong-Kong—only eight days' passage. The mainmast was found to be quite rotten; and, as there was a little difficulty in getting a spar to suit, I suggested that we should take the foremast for the mainmast, and a line-of-battle ship's maintopmast for a foremast, which answers admirably, and I think the little vessel is all the better for her masts being reduced. We left all our guns but two, and that heavy pinnace, at Hong-Kong. The latter stows snugly amidships, and we are as comfortable as we possibly can be. The Admiral was uncommonly kind, and has written a very flattering letter to the Admiralty about me. He gave us a capital refit—all new lower rigging from the Hercules' gear. Our old rigging, when we came to strip it, was found to be quite gone; there was not a shroud which was not stranded in the eye: fortunately we did not fall in with very bad weather, or we must have lost our masts. I wish we could have come down to your part of the world before going home; it would have given us all the greatest possible pleasure, and I know, old fellow, what your feelings would be on the occasion. That fellow, Mr ——, whom you recollect I gave my cabin up to when he had the small-pox, not only gave me the disease (which he could not help), but has let me in for a £21 bill. I think it is the height of ingratitude; don't you? God bless you, my dear fellow." And at the top of the letter he writes—"For we are homeward bound, my boys, for we are homeward bound."

On the passage he was constantly occupied with his charts, reducing into shape and form the vast multitude of "observations" which he had amassed during the Survey. Now arrived at the "Scilly Light," he addressed his old messmate, of date *23d May* 1854, thus:—"The little vessel at last actually within 100 miles of old England!!! Almost every day I have said to myself—'I will begin a letter to P——;' and, as usual with me, I have put it off until we are almost in such a bustle as to prevent me writing to you at all. Millman is hard at work opposite to me, copying all my official letters, which also have been delayed to the last moment. But you must not infer from this that I have been idle; quite the contrary, I assure you; for we have been able to work at the charts the greater part of the voyage. Sailing from Singapore (where I wrote to you last) on the 17th of January, we ran with a fresh breeze through the Rhio Strait that night—rather anxious work, as it was pitch-dark, and the vessel with all studding-sails going about eight knots. Thanks, however, to the same Providence which has watched over us so often before, we cleared all dangers and got well to sea by the following morning. Thence we steered to pass through the Strait of Banca, running over the positions of one or two reported dangers without picking them up (which, by the way, did not perplex me much, as we have had quite enough of that sort of work), and entered the strait early in the morning. Running through the strait with the most delightful breeze and clear weather, we anchored just at its southern entrance at ten the same night. Out again at daylight, and arrived at Anger at noon the next day.

"My dear P——," he continues, "you cannot imagine what an extraordinary feeling came over me; running night after night, studding-sails 'low and aloft, with actually a *chart* (upon which, however, only a small amount of reliance could be placed) to go by!! was something so unusual that I went to bed at night with an idea that a feather-bed in Windsor Castle could not be more secure; and yet this is a sea which causes so much anxiety to new-comers. It only shews what creatures of habit we are. Well, as usual, all the way down, we were promising ourselves what a delightful little trip on shore we should have at Anger; and when we came to realise it, we found by far the greatest pleasure had been in the anticipation, for a more miserable, dull, stupid, but very pretty little hole we agreed we had never seen before. There is no hotel there now, and we actually went into the cocoanut plantation on the left of the village, to lie down and kill time whilst the vessel was watering, the pic-nic coming off ultimately at my cabin-table. We sailed at daylight the following morning for Mew Bay, where I wanted to swing the ship, not having been able to do it when at Singapore in consequence of a heavy ground-swell which set into the Roads all the time we were there. I suppose you know Mew Bay and the beautiful waterfall? We had all the ship's company on shore under it, to give themselves and clothes a good cleansing before starting on our long sea-voyage to the Cape, where fresh water would be a scarce article. We were all in such high spirits: you would hear one chap say—his face and body covered with soap-suds, and giving an extra rub and blow as he uttered it—'I say, Bill, you 'd better make the most of it; you won't get this this day fortnight;' and indeed they did not, nor the officers either, for we were all at the time predicted upon three quarts. Having swung the ship, we weighed, and took our departure from Java Head at 6 P.M. with a delightfully fresh S.E. trade and clear weather. I shall never forget how free from anxiety I went to bed that night, with *cables unbent* and no breast-ropes in the chains!! separated from all coral reefs by the island of Java, with the long rolling ocean-swell deprived of its terrors in consequence."

Suddenly interrupted in his narrative by the pressure of occupation, we find him "sailing into Portsmouth harbour under double-reefed topsails—as much as the vessel could carry, and running at once alongside the jetty. We cleared off everything," he writes to the same friend, "and were paid off in one week after our arrival,—masts out and ballast stacked. The officers said they had seldom seen a man-of-war pay off so clean and well. We had not a man drunk. Every person, from the Commander-in-chief downwards, who saw the little vessel was very much pleased with her appearance and cleanly condition. She certainly looked well, and very clean." And thus ended an arduous service of five years, nine months of every twelve of which he had spent "out of the pale of civilisation."

On his arrival, he not unnaturally looked for a prompt recognition of his great services. He had executed an elaborate Hydrographic Survey of an island three hundred miles long, with its harbours and adjacent waters, fixing all the mountains and prominent hills visible from the sea. He had been "strongly recommended" for promotion by the successive Admirals under whom he served, the last only withholding it because he "believed it would certainly be given by the home-authorities." But "he returned to England," says Captain Collinson, "only again to be subjected to official routine; for, though highly commended by the different Commanders-in-chief for the praiseworthy manner in which he had performed the onerous duty imposed on him, as well as for the admirable discipline maintained in his vessel, he was told there was no promotion for him except through the Hydrographer, who has a captain's vacancy at his disposal every second year."

The neglect, however, did not cast him down. It was noticed that in his absence a peculiar heavenliness had settled upon him, as if, whilst

"Walking by the sea, beneath the gentle stars,"

not a few "kindling seeds" of holiness had "sprouted within his soul." The writer well remembers that calm and heavenly mien, and the unmurmuring patience of his manly but meek spirit during those two dreary years. He felt the neglect, and felt it bitterly; but the rod was in the hand of his Father in heaven, and the discipline was quickly ripening him for the glory he was so soon to enter.

CHAPTER IX.

"Thy tried and lonely spirit
Thirsts for the living God,
And pleads alone the merit
Of rich, redeeming blood.

"Take up a song of gladness
While smarting 'neath the rod;
Triumphant over sadness,
Witness before thy God."

"WILL you, each of you, make it a special subject of *prayer* for direction as to the course I should pursue? Then, come what will, I know it will be well." Such were Bate's words to his sisters, on returning from the Admiralty one afternoon in January (1856), not a little perplexed as to the way of duty. After occupying many months in completing his charts and in compiling sailing-directions for them, he had been allowed to exchange from the Surveying-department into the general service, in the hope of working out more speedily his promotion; and, receiving soon afterwards a nomination to the Mariner in the West Indies, he had gone down to Whitehall to take up his appointment, when a vacancy which had just occurred in the command of the Bittern—a vessel of sixteen guns, stationed in the Chinese waters—was unexpectedly offered to him, with only two days to decide. Neither position was at all such as he had a right to expect; but, unwilling to remain longer idle, he chose the Bittern, and at once prepared to set out.

Before following him on his new and (as it proved) his last expedition, we revert for a moment to the months which he had spent in England since his return in the Royalist to Portsmouth. "After my arrival," we find him writing from London, in November 1855, to the same dear friend in Australia, "we were paid off; Calver, Bullock, and myself were put on the Fisgard's books; but I was allowed to take rooms at Mr Gillott's, 36 Strand, to get our work up. This occupied us till the end of October. Calver and Bullock were promoted on my recommendation immediately they passed; and I received a complimentary letter on putting the charts into office. The west coast of Palawan was done on one inch; and, to make the thing complete, and appear all in one, we projected the east coast on the same sheets, and gave the whole island in on the inch plan. It looked uncommonly well when put together, the edge of the bank of soundings all being included. Malampaya Sound was done on three inches, and extended from Bacuit to Wedge Island, an enormous but beautiful plan, all so elaborately worked out. Separate plans are also made, on a scale of two inches, of the coast to the southward (where, you recollect, all the islands are) as far as Ooloogan Bay. Royal Captain, Bombay, Half-moon, and other shoals were laid down on four inches, and put in their new positions on the triangulation sheet (which was a *long* roll of paper), on the scale of one-third of an inch, graduated in latitude and longitude. Sketches also from various positions on the edge of the bank were given in; and, last of all, the 'Sailing Directions, and General Description of Palawan.' The latter is published in the new edition of Horsburgh; and, *for the paper,* the proprietors have made me a present of the Work—more civil than the Admiralty have been.

"And now," he continues in the same letter, "as to promotion. The Hydrographic Office and Admiralty have arranged that there shall be *one step* given in the year to the scientific branch of the service. Whether it be a captain or commander, I don't know. Last year, however, it was a captain's commission which was given; and it was *bestowed on one of the old home-surveyors.* It remains to be seen what they will do this year. The Hydrographer, who received me *most kindly,* told me that, if it had been in his power, he would have given me my commission the day I put my charts into office. But look at his practice. The Government might as well say (comparing small things with great) to the young fellows in the Crimea who have taken Sebastopol—'Yes, we admit you have done your work well, and deserve promotion; but there are some old officers who have been serving a long time in the depôt at home, that must have the few vacancies which are at our disposal.' If foreign surveyors are to compete in standing with home ones, I must wait till I am grey-headed. However, if I do not get it this year, 'Good-bye, H.O.,' say I. I have already been making applications for service in the general line, and hope never more to have a word to say to the H.O. Surveying-department. I wrote to W—— how useful your quintant had been; and he has, I believe, purchased it. I only returned to London on Saturday, after a five months' cruise, and don't know yet for certain what he has given for it. It is difficult to get them to move in any shape,—the war absorbs all attention, and fills every office with working material."

Referring to an "unfortunate affair" which a captain of a ship had had with his officers, he proceeds:—

"I have only heard one side of the story (and that's his), and am therefore not in a position to pass judgment. At the same time, I cannot but believe, from certain facts which were brought to my notice, that nothing could justify certain particulars in their conduct. They quarrelled amongst themselves, and, in the bitterness of their anger, appear to have lost all self-respect. My dear P——, they lacked the one thing needful; and that is the reason things went to the extent they did. It is (I am as sure of it as that I am now writing) as impossible for a body of human beings to be boxed up together for one twelvemonth, with no genuine religious principle to actuate their every-day conduct (let alone thoughts), and not quarrel, as it is for a Chinaman to tell the truth, or for you to love dishonesty. Bad as my example was in the Royalist, there was a little religious principle in thought, if not in action, which in the long run leavened the viler part of my nature. Poor dear —— was far above me in amiability of temper, and in the other qualities which ennoble man: but then he had not a religious man second in command, and there is where I was more fortunate than he. I care not who the man is. If he have no spirituality of mind, he is not to be trusted when difficult questions arise. The more I live in the world, the more convinced I am of this. Look at the conduct of the noble and great of the land!! Oh! what littleness have some—indeed I may say, all—displayed since the pressure of war has been put upon them! In proportion as we discharge our duty faithfully as unto God, and not unto man, so shall we find comfort when men speak ill of us. —— was most anxious for a court-martial; and I urged it all I could, because reports so prejudicial to his character had gone abroad, that I thought it necessary and right that the whole truth, and nothing but the truth, should be made public, in order either to counteract or confirm them. Let every one stand or fall by their own conduct, whether they be brother, father, sister, or mother—I care not whom."

And he adds:—"Is there any chance of yet coming home? I should very much like to meet you again, if the Lord will. It is a comfort to know and *feel* that our pilgrimage here is in the hands of the Lord:

after all, it matters little whether we meet on earth, so long as we are sure of being with each other throughout the endless ages of eternity,—our wives, our families, our friends, all together, with nothing to interrupt their happiness. M'Clure is knighted, and has received £5000. If I am not promoted at the end of the year, I cut the H.O., and try for employment in the regular line. I often wish I were married, and quietly settled for life. It is all vanity and vexation of spirit. If I had enough to keep a wife, I would throw up my commission, and live quietly, making myself as useful to my fellow-creatures as I could. God bless you, my dear P——." And this postscript follows:—"I received such a nice letter from C——, who is now in the Sphinx. God has enlightened him with His Holy Spirit, and he *sees beyond this life.*"

Another day, about the same period, he addressed a friend at home thus:—"I hope you do not think, because I have not written to you before, that you have not had my sympathy in your sufferings. I was indeed sorry for your accident, but very, very thankful at the same time, that you escaped as you did. It is a comfort to feel that there is a 'why' and a 'wherefore' in all the dispensations of God's providence, and that He doeth all things well, however adverse they may appear at the time. I thank God I dislocated my shoulder, because it humbled me, and I feel it has done me good."

In the month of January following he received the appointment already named, and he lost no time in getting ready. It was the last glimpse which his friends were to have of him; and it almost seemed as if a presentiment had taken possession of him that he should "see their face no more." They remember now a certain indescribable solemnity which marked those parting hours. Not accustomed to *say* much, he yet had a parting word for each.

"Thank —— for her kind message," he wrote to one; "I shall indeed esteem it a great privilege to be remembered by her at the throne of grace; and I do pray she may never forget me in her supplications to God, for no one needs more than I do God's grace to walk uprightly in His commandments. If you will do the same, I shall indeed feel grateful."

And to another:—"But, after all, it does not much matter whether we meet in this world or not. The great end we must *all* have in view is a glorious union hereafter, where that painful word 'Good-bye' is never heard, and where one's brains and wretched body which we carry about with us here shall be no longer subject to torment and disease."

And to a third, thus:—"What a comfort, in this your sad trial, to be able to recognise the hand of a good and gracious Father! However severe the chastening may be, one thing I feel certain of, that you will hereafter, if you do not in the fullest sense *now*, thank God with all your heart and soul that He thus visited you. You know you will. God bless you! If it be good for you, may you have a speedy recovery! and if not, may you realise—what is far better than health—that full and perfect measure of God's grace which enables *all* to rejoice in tribulation!"

These were no mere words of course. Uttered by *him*, they meant much. He was administering from the deep well-spring of his heart the consolations with which he had himself been so richly comforted of God.

It was on a bright morning in the early spring that he bade a last adieu to the shores of old England. "Left Portsmouth," he writes, "by the 8.15 A.M. train for Southampton; at 9.50 were hauled into the fair-way; and, at 12, a small steam-tender left the dock for the Avon with passengers. Went off; saw my cabin; and, after depositing my baggage, returned and sauntered about the shore till the tender took her final departure with the mails. Walked about the docks with E——d and P——, and at 2.30 took my final leave of the shore and of those dear to me." In his sister's Bible, he marked the following texts:—1 Thess. iv. 18; 2 Thess. iii. 16; Numb. vi. 26. His last words, on parting, were—"PRAY FOR ME."

The voyage out was not very prolific of incidents; but we select from his diary a few wayfarer's notes, as a specimen of his daily routine:—

"*Feb.* 4, 1856. The mails being delivered over, consisting of 873 boxes and 44 bags, we slipped the buoy at 3.10 P.M. At 5.20 passed Hurst Castle: 5.47, passed the Needles.

"*Feb.* 5. Average speed of the vessel, 9½ and 10 knots; making 26¾ revolutions. Noon: Heavy westerly swell. The majority of the passengers below sea-sick: not a lady on deck. Midnight: Strong breeze from the S.W. increasing together with the sea. Vessel beginning to make all hands feel as if they wished they had never put foot afloat.

"*Feb.* 6. Strong breeze all night. Inclined to freshen; although the barometer does not lead one to apprehend a gale. Sea increasing. Passengers crawling about in a miserable condition. The Companion seems a favourite place for them to huddle together: they get out of the wet there, and enjoy the fresh air at the same time. Unfortunately for them, it is contrary to the regulations *in all ships* for any one to monopolise a thoroughfare. A notice was placed up somewhat to that effect; and the poor fellows had to seek, some their beds, some *anywhere*, and some no doubt wished they were overboard. Noon: Heavy sea from the S.W. Ship pitching, and taking in much water over all. Down masts and yards."

The day following, towards the afternoon, the weather moderated, "to the great delight of the passengers," who "were of opinion that no gale could have been worse." And the next morning he writes:—"Some of the young passengers are walking six inches taller already, having weathered 'one of the heaviest gales that was ever known;' and he who has not once been sea-sick is indeed a hero. For my own part, I am uncommonly glad it is over. I was in bed all Wednesday, feeling wretchedly uncomfortable. One or two of the ladies have appeared on deck; but they have all suffered very severely. At midnight, made Bayonne

Light. Moderate and fine. The Band plays for an hour in the Saloon every evening."

On *Feb.* 11, the vessel anchored off Gibraltar. "The steward," he says, "gave passes for a passage to and from the shore, at the rate of 2d. for each person. Visited the Galleries and a portion of the neutral ground. Breakfasted at the hotel. Gibraltar derives its name from the Moorish general by whom it was captured in 711. It remained in possession of the Moors till the fourteenth century, when the Spaniards took it; but they lost it again in 1333, and retook it 1462. Sir George Rook captured the place on 24th July 1704; since which time it has remained in possession of the English, despite the various attempts on the part of the French and Spaniards to wrest it from them."

As they were nearing Malta, he wrote another old brother officer, *Feb.* 14, thus:—"These screw-ships are horridly inconvenient vessels for writing in. They vibrate fore and aft like a person with a fit of 'shakes.' After leaving Ushant, we had a hard blow from the S.W. which lasted four days. The vessel knocked about terribly, and made me very ill for one day. We arrived at Gibraltar on Monday the 11th, and I had a four hours' cruise over the place. The Galleries are wonderful; but, as for the rest of the place, I would not live in it for £1000 a-year. It is not unlike Hong-Kong, viewing a certain portion of it from seaward, and, in the summer, must be quite equal to it for heat. We expect to get into Malta to-morrow morning. Since entering the Mediterranean, we have had the most lovely weather, the thermometer never ranging higher than 65°. The captain is a good officer, and conducts the duties of the ship in a very quiet, gentleman-like style. We are particularly fortunate in our passengers; they appear to be a very nice set; the *ladies* even have not quarrelled. The time passes very pleasantly and quickly."

We next find him off Alexandria:—"*Feb.* 19. Made the light (fixed bright light), the highest object in the vicinity of the harbour, at a quarter before midnight. The night was remarkably fine; and the moon and stars shone brilliantly. Closed the light, and then hauled off under easy steam till daylight. Shortly after daylight, the Pilot came off, and conducted her safely to the anchorage at 7 o'clock. The passengers had an early breakfast at half-past 7; immediately after which we landed as best we could in boats belonging to the shore. An omnibus took us to the Hôtel d'Europe, near the S.E. angle of the Great Square. And at 10.30 we started for the railway station, which is about two miles out of the town."

In the Gulf of Suez, he writes:—"*Feb.* 24. Ship under all sail. Average speed from 10½ to 11 knots; revolutions from 26 to 27. Divine service was performed in the saloon: majority of passengers attended. The Rev. Mr Ottley preached. Service in the saloon in the evening: Mr H—— expounded a portion of Scripture. Lamentable to see how few of the passengers attended." Then, *Feb.* 27, he says:—"Passengers employed variously. Eating, drinking, and sleeping appear to be their chief occupation."

Another day:—"*Feb.* 29. At 4 A.M. we were off Mecca. At 10, passed through the Strait of Babelmandeb. Between Babelmandeb and Aden the shore is generally low, with a sandy level. At the back is a remarkable high range of mountains, the summit of which is broken into sharp peaks of a curious configuration. We could trace no signs of inhabitants, nor of villages of any kind, on the shore. At 10 we anchored in three fathoms, off the coaling settlement. The Oriental had just arrived with the homeward-bound passengers from India. She had one or two cases of small-pox on board, which created a little alarm amongst the passengers. The patients were landed immediately and received into hospital. Sleep was out of the question, all the ports being closed in consequence of coaling, which was most suffocating."

And, the day following, he adds:—"Breakfasted on shore. As usual, the majority of the passengers started off for the cantonment, while the remainder contented themselves with lounging about the hotel. Aden is a vile hole; and, if they who are compelled to live in it have no resources within themselves, they must pass a miserable existence indeed. Aden, or 'Portus Romanus,' as it was formerly called, was fortified by the Turkish sultan, Solyman the Magnificent. It was afterwards held by the Arab Sheikhs of the surrounding district, and subsequently fell into the hands of the East India Company, having been taken by assault in 1839 by a combined naval and military force. We weighed at 1.30 P.M."

A week later, he writes:—"*March* 9. The forenoon was calm and sultry; not a breath of air was stirring except what the vessel created by her own velocity. Divine service was performed on deck under an awning. Mr —— preached. He certainly is not one of St Paul's men. Several fishing-boats were about; and on one island was a small village, built apparently of timber. Porpoises and gulls were very numerous. The sea was like glass; and at one time we could not have had less than eight or ten islands in view. By 4 P.M. we had passed well through them."

And March 10:—"Thermometer 85° throughout the night; and not a breath of wind to disturb the glassy surface of the sea. Employed copying a letter Mrs Wauchope gave me, being extracts from one Lady Agnew wrote, giving an account of Annie Agnew's illness and sweet deathbed. What a lovely testimony did she give to the truth and power of God's Word!—When thou passest through 'the valley of the shadow of death,' 'I will be with thee.'"

Other two days brought him to Point de Galle. "At daybreak," he writes, "we weighed, and steamed into the bay. Depositing my chronometers on board the Madras, I landed with Mrs Wauchope, Gibson, and party. He went to the Mansion-house Hotel for the purpose of taking breakfast; but, while there, Mr Stewart of the Peninsular and Oriental Company prevailed on us to take a drive of four miles into the country to a place called the Gardens, where he had ordered breakfast to be laid in a deliciously cool bungalow situated on the summit of a hill commanding a most delightful view of the surrounding country. We returned at noon, and embarked all together, the Bengal portion of our party coming on board to see the accommodation the Madras afforded. At 2 P.M. the two steamers weighed, and proceeded on their voyage."

On March 19, he says:—"At about 5 P.M. we passed close to Pulo Perda, which is a round rocky islet, about 200 feet above the sea, covered apparently with guano, and not a vestige of vegetation visible. It lies about eighty miles from Penang." And the day following:—"Soon after midnight, we saw the island of Penang, bearing south-east. At 2 we received a pilot; and at 4.30 we anchored off the town. The Bishop of Calcutta arrived this morning in the Hooghly: he was saluted on landing. Wrote a hurried letter to E——d after breakfast, and then went on shore to take a drive into the country. Sir Benson Maxwell was sworn into office under a salute of guns. He embarked for Singapore, to hold a conference with the Governor relative to the new charter for organising separate courts of judicature at Penang and Singapore. Received the China mail, and left the harbour at 1 P.M."

The next day, at dusk, they were off Malacca; and, the day following, at 11.30, they anchored at Singapore. He writes:—"H.M.S. Encounter, just arrived from Calcutta, was here; also the American frigate Macedonian, and French frigate Constantine, and a small 14-gun brig. The two latter vessels were co-operating with our squadron in the Gulf of Tartary last year. Captain, or Commodore (for he had his pendant flying), Montravel speaks English tolerably well. He passed a high eulogium on the characters of the British officers commanding the ships on the Castries Bay expedition, and appeared to think there was no blame attributable to Commodore Elliott in not attacking the Russian squadron on that occasion. The Commander-in-chief's inactivity appeared to be more the subject of censure. Dined in the country, about three miles away, with Mr and Mrs Harvey, and slept on board the steamer."

Before leaving Singapore, he was gladdened with a letter from his old shipmate, resident at Victoria, New South Wales, in answer to one from himself before leaving England. We quote a few sentences as illustrative of the character of his friendships:— "Your letter came in, about three hours since, while we were at dinner. When we first opened the parcel with your letter, and saw a book, I thought it might possibly be the 'Royalist's Voyage,' or 'Account of Palawan,' with the author's affectionate regards. Is there any chance of such a work? I can imagine your feeling of satisfaction on seeing both coasts of Palawan snugly on one sheet. I long to see them out. You ask, my dear Bate, what is the most useful thing you can send your godchild, our dear boy. My wife and I were both struck with your generous offer, and agree that the most valuable gift we can suggest, and which we are sure will be the most lasting in benefit to the child, is, your fervent prayers to our heavenly Father that he may be *indeed* His own child—that he may be lifted out of the mire of the flesh, and his feet set upon the Rock of Ages—his going established in the narrow path, and the new song put into his mouth. This is asking the most we could, yet in the confidence we are not asking too much of you and yours. He will be two years old, if he is permitted to continue with us, on the 6th of April next—chatters very intelligibly—and is just beginning to lisp his prayers on his mother's knee. That is the most lovely sight in nature. I wish you could enjoy it with me. I suppose you have seen Lady Parry and her family since dear Sir Edward's death."

On March 23, he sailed from Singapore for Hong-Kong. "As Jardine's steamer, the Fiery Cross," he writes, "had arrived the previous evening, and was about to leave for China immediately, we put all steam up in this vessel, and managed, notwithstanding the foul state of her bottom, to get 8¼ knots and 22½ revolutions. The Fiery Cross is said to be very fast; and great fears are entertained that she will be before this vessel in the opium market. Both ships are loaded with the drug. The Malwa, of Bombay production, is said to fetch the most in the China market. The Chinese themselves grow a little; but, notwithstanding

M. Huc's assertion to the contrary, it is inferior to our Patna, which, I believe, is considered to be the worst kind imported into China. We have a thousand chests on board, the value of each one of which is four hundred dollars when landed at Hong-Kong. The profit must be enormous, when these are sold to the Chinese at the rate of eight hundred dollars per chest,—ah! and are caught up by them with the greatest avidity."

One or two little incidents are noted, as he proceeds:—"*March* 24. On examining the boxes of the Chinese on board belonging to the ship, as much as 12,000 dollars were found amongst them. Freightage was charged forthwith, at which they were a little astonished." And, March 25:—"By our reckoning we passed five miles from the Charlotte Bank about 4 o'clock. It is not a danger likely to bring a vessel up, by all accounts; although I believe the only authority we have for this is Horsburgh. I know no person who has actually run his ship over it; though until closely questioned, many say they have. When captains out here tell you they have passed over shoals, as a general rule never believe them."

Two days later, he writes:—"They are so very reluctant to spread the awnings on board this ship for fear of being overtaken by the Fiery Cross, that by 12 o'clock the vessel becomes so heated throughout as to make it next to impossible to sit down to do anything requiring attention. Thus we pay, in discomfort, for the small satisfaction of the chance of not being outstript in our voyage by an opposition-vessel!"

On March 30:—"We experienced a sudden change this morning. At daylight, it blew fresh with drenching rain and a head-sea, which made most of the passengers feel very uncomfortable, myself among the number. Several junks in sight, some of which we passed very close to. At 6.30, we came to an anchor off West Point, it being too dark to proceed further, with the harbour so full of shipping. At 8, went on board the Winchester in the guard-boat, to call upon the Admiral. Bittern not yet arrived, but expected hourly."

"*April* 1. Called, during the day, on the Bishop and some others of my old friends. Much to my regret, I found the Rev. Mr Morton had, in consequence of ill health, been obliged to abandon his post at Loo-choo. He has been living for some months with the Bishop, the French frigate Sybille having kindly brought him over. How mysterious are the ways of God! Mr M. had just succeeded in accomplishing the language, and could speak fluently to the natives: he felt his position on the island secure: the Government had in a measure ceased to oppose him in his mission-work: and yet, for some wise purpose hereafter to be revealed to us, God sees fit to remove him at the very moment when we thought everything was going on so prosperously. He certainly looks very unwell; and medical men here say he ought not to return to Loo-choo." "The Loo-chooian Government has taken charge of the house and property belonging to the Mission; and, on Mr Morton delivering it over to them, one of the agents expressed a wish that he would soon return. Mr M. gave them to understand, that, if he himself did not, another missionary would very shortly. The French Jesuits have now entire charge of the spiritual welfare of the poor Loochooians. This is very distressing; but it is a comfort to feel that God can accomplish His own purposes, however strangely to us He may appear to go to work about it."

"*April* 2. No Bittern yet! A report is about, that she is at Amoy. If she have a large convoy to bring down, she will probably, by the dilatoriness of the Chinese, be some days before she makes her appearance. Walked to East Point. The population of Hong-Kong and influx of inhabitants are increasing rapidly. Houses are building in every direction; but more particularly in the district known as Typing-shan, the scene of a terrible conflagration about two years since, where poor Lieutenant Luff, R.A., lost his life, and Lieutenant Wilson of the Engineers was so frightfully wounded and burnt. Met Captain Parker and the Rev. J. Irwin, Colonial Chaplain, at dinner at the Bishop's in the evening."

"*April* 5. Took a walk with Captain Parker, and met at his house in the evening at dinner a German missionary, Mr Lobchild. Mr L. related some most interesting anecdotes relative to his mission. He lives in a small village about forty miles north of this, enjoying perfect security, although exposed at times to some perils whilst interposing and mediating between parties who are frequently at war with each other. They have no less than eight stations, and I believe number among them about five hundred converts. Mr L. has about sixty in his district; and he believes them to be sincere. One great test, he says, is, when they give up the worship of their ancestors, a custom (Huc confirms this) to which, of all others, they are most addicted, money-making perhaps excepted."

At length, on April 7, his ship arrived; and, a day or two afterwards, he took the command.

CHAPTER X.

> "Oh! check the reckless murmur ever rising still,
> Which proves that *Thine* is not Thy servant's only will.
> I long for Thee, my Saviour! Even in this dark day,
> From Thee proceeds the only bright or cheering ray."

"Let me hear from you," wrote a friend to him, "how ever you accepted the command of such a paltry brig. But doubtless the Lord has directed you, and in your present position you have *His* work to do. May you have grace abundantly to accomplish His purposes!" All his friends were chagrined and pained. "The vessel," says an officer who held a command in the Chinese waters, "had been so much damaged, that she was really not sea-worthy." But Bate was not a man to mope over his ill-treatment. He was in the place where God had put him; and he steadfastly set his face to his work, caring only to approve himself to his Master in heaven.

After docking at Whampoa, the Bittern was at length put into repair; and her commander gradually communicated to the ship's company that high tone of discipline which his firm hand and kind heart never failed to impart. At first, if the men were allowed of a Sunday afternoon to have a country ramble, they "abused the indulgence by returning, more than half of them, drunk;" but a few weeks had not passed when "all the liberty-men, with the exception of three, came on board to time and quite sober." His method of dealing with them is instructive.

On April 27, he writes:—"Performed divine service on deck. Commenced the plan of reading a sermon (one of Mr Molyneux's short ones, 'Broken Bread') to the men. They don't quite understand what I am after. I trust God will give me grace to continue it, and, as soon as the vessel is a little more settled, to have daily prayer also. I think their spiritual concerns have been made subordinate to their temporal affairs."

And, a week or two later, he says:—"Performed divine service on the lower deck. Read a sermon to the men: 2d Chapter of Doddridge's 'Rise and Progress.' I wonder if any effect was produced. Some appeared attentive; others perfectly indifferent. O God! I pray that Thy Word, even when uttered by such a vile instrument as Thou hast chosen, may go forth with power to the hearts of my hearers, and that it may not return unto Thee void, but that it may accomplish the work whereunto Thou hast sent it. Let Thy Spirit do His full work, I pray Thee, amongst the seamen and marines of this ship. Truly it may be said that darkness covers the ship, and gross darkness her company."

And, on Monday, May 19, he adds:—"After quarters this morning, I told the ship's company it was my intention to establish a custom of reading a portion of Scripture, and offering up one or two prayers in public acknowledgment of what we all ought individually to feel—the boundless goodness and merciful providence of God. The announcement appeared to be well received; and I commenced forthwith by reading the first chapter of John, and concluding with our Lord's Prayer and the prayer used at sea. May God give me grace and strength to continue this duty!"

A blessing attended—as it always does—the work of faith and of love. A few weeks afterwards, writing to a friend in England respecting it, he says:—"I have established morning-prayers; and on Sundays I am told the attention of the men is more than it has ever been before. I read a chapter in the Bible—not a long one—every morning after divisions, and conclude with the Lord's Prayer and one or two extempore prayers. I think it answers well: the fellows are happy; and so am I." And he adds:—"Last Sunday, I commenced reading Molyneux's 'World to Come,' in the hope the subject would interest both officers and men. I purpose (*D.V.*) going through with it. I spoke to my men about the Nightingale Fund; and they have one and all contributed two days' pay."

The truth is, his own daily walk was so transparently holy, and his manly face so beamed with kindness, that his men felt themselves unconsciously attracted to HIM whose service their beloved commander so evidently felt to be "perfect freedom." "The fellows are happy, and so am I." Such is the secret of every endeavour which has on it the stamp of God's approval.

> "Go to, ye careless mockers,
> Despise it as ye will,
> There *is* a truth and power
> In Christ's religion still.
> No more ideal day-dreams
> The true believer hath,
> There is a secret brightness
> Which shines around his path.
> There is a life, and unction,
> A vivid, holy joy,
> A love within his bosom,
> No waters can destroy!"

Like Havelock, he combined with his anxiety for the spiritual welfare of his men, a strict, unflinching discipline. On the occasion already named, when three of the "liberty-men" returned intoxicated, he writes:—"One of the three is a quartermaster, the oldest and best sailor in the ship. This blackguard does all the mischief. It is my intention to flog one of them to-morrow." And the next day, accordingly, he records:—"Punished J. Wilson with a dozen strokes of the 'cat.'"

And, a week or two later, he writes:—"Read the Articles of War, and took a 'good-conduct badge' away from the boatswain's mate for drunkenness and insubordination. He has been sixteen years in the service, and had three stripes. I question if they are well merited. He was one of the first men I saw lying dead-drunk under Mr Cowper's shed on the Sunday night when so many of the ship's company were intoxicated."

And, two days later:—"Sent an officer and party with the master-at-arms of H.M.S. Nankin away early this morning, to board the English ships lying in the river, in search of deserters. None were found afloat; but on entering a boarding-house in Bamboo-town, they surprised six of them, though they only succeeded in capturing three. The remainder, leaving their clothes behind, escaped into the country."

His discipline was not the arbitrary and repulsive caprice of the martinet, but the calm and winning considerateness of the Christian man. "One could see in a moment," says a friend (the Rev. John Irwin, M.A., Colonial Chaplain) whose hospitality he often enjoyed at this period, "the remarkable attachment of his officers and ship's company to him. He had in a strong degree the power of attaching to him all who were under his command, and of inspiring them with confidence in him. I remember accompanying him in a visit to the hospital-ship; and, in going amongst the sick, he recognised one or two of his former ship's company who had been with him in the Royalist. I was struck with the way in which they mutually greeted each other as old friends, the eyes of the poor invalids brightening up as they listened to his words of kindness and consolation.

"From all quarters," adds the same friend, "there were testimonies to his extraordinary consideration for those under his command. He remarked to me one day, that he always found kindness the most effectual way of dealing with men of all classes and dispositions.

'We are sure,' said he, 'to do wrong what we do in a passion. I once punished a man hastily and in a passion, and I did wrong.' The circumstances were, as I remember, that, returning on board the Royalist at night, and one of the hands being reported by an officer for insubordination, he had ordered him to be punished on the spot, and afterwards he had reason to believe that he had acted unjustly as well as hastily."

Another glimpse into his daily routine at this time is given in a letter to his sisters, dated "H.M.S. Bittern, Whampoa, June 1st (1856)," thus:—"My dearest Girls, The thermometer now whilst I am writing is 88½°; it is a dead calm; and really I can scarcely muster sufficient resolution and energy to go on with this letter—only I know, if I do not commence at once, affairs will get worse instead of better. The hot season is just commencing; and if this be the earnest of what we are to expect for the next three months, why, I wish I was at the North Pole. Sleeping at night is out of the question; for, in addition to the heat, one is obliged to be enveloped in mosquito-curtains to prevent being eaten alive. I get up in the morning completely fatigued from my *night's rest.* I am delighted to hear such good accounts of dear M——. Thank God for it. Mr H—— is an honest man to refund without being asked: I suspect one half your London tailors would have remained silent about it. I hear the Admiral has recommended the Bittern to be sold out here, and that the officers and ship's company should go home in the Winchester. Since I last wrote, I had a visit from him. He is very kind; and I liked him much—what little I saw of him. He left it to myself whether I would go and lie off Canton or remain at Whampoa. I preferred the latter place, as it is much more healthy and a great deal cooler. At Canton now the heat is insufferable, even in the factories; on board ship it would be ten times worse. I am positively dripping even now with perspiration.

"The Admiral," he continues, "sails on the 11th for the four ports. He will also visit Castries Bay, and deliver over the prisoners of war to the Russian authorities at the Amour. If the Bittern had been sound, we would probably have gone with him; for he said to me how much he felt the vessel being obliged to lay up in the Canton River, having a Commander on board her distinguished in the Surveying service—or words to that effect. It is not improbable I may come home overland: however, you will know my fate before I do. We are now busy painting and putting the vessel in order: she is a beautiful thing—a regular little man-of-war. The ship's company are very good, on the whole; rather noisy, and some few inclined to drink. However, with all the temptation laid in their way, and thorough disorganisation consequent on docking, I have been able, with the assistance of my first lieutenant, to bring them round without much punishment. You can't imagine how thin I am getting. I never take any wine but Claret and Hock, and that very seldom; and, as for beer, I don't think I have drunk three bottles since I left England. I usually go on shore for a walk about five P.M., I come on board to a *meat-tea* at seven." And, after some further details, he closes characteristically, thus:—"God bless you, dears! Ever your loving—WILL."

Whilst waiting for the Admiral's orders respecting his destination, he made occasional visits to the town and neighbouring country. "This Whampoa," he wrote one day, "is a detestable hole, abounding with every species of villany and vice. There is a 'Sing-song' or Chinese play going on, some two or three times in the week. It attracts people from all parts of the island, and some from the neighbouring shore. The women appear to take peculiar delight in it. I believe the actors generally wind up with some drama in which the grossest obscenity is represented." And, another day, he says:—"The Chinese here are the greatest set of rascals under the sun; and the women are twice as bad—up to any amount of villany."

And, another day, he wrote:—"Went on shore at five this morning to take a walk; and, returning along the bank of the creek which separates Bamboo-town from a village east of it, I discovered, at the entrance, on the left bank, the body of a native lying upon his belly, frightfully lacerated about the head and left arm especially, groaning and at times writhing in agony. The Chinese were standing round him, totally unconcerned, the *women* laughing at his sufferings. The man was quite insensible, except to pain. With some difficulty, I procured a small litter, for which I promised to pay one dollar, and brought him alongside this vessel, with a view to procure surgical assistance and perchance save a life which, alas! appeared to be fast ebbing. The unfortunate man was not stript of any of his clothing; but his knife had been taken from the leathern sheath which he carried about his person. By the time I reached the ship, his spirit had well-nigh departed; and the doctor's assistance was of no avail. One or two convulsions of the throat and thorax, and he was no more. He belonged to the Peninsular and Oriental Steamer Chusan, now lying here. The vice-consul, with a jury of three merchant-captains, held an inquest on the body; and I went on board the Alligator to give my evidence respecting the discovery of the unfortunate creature. I will be bound to say a woman had, either directly or indirectly, something to do with the murder."

A few days later, an incident occurred, which he narrates thus:—"The captain of a lorcha, flying English colours but owned by Chinese, came on board to tell us that his life was in danger, being apprehensive that the crew intended rising against his authority when below the Bogue forts, for the purpose of plundering the vessel of the six thousand dollars with which she was partly laden, and of then taking her up the coast on a piratical cruise. He had two Europeans on board, picked up at Whampoa last night, whom he had thought to get to protect him against the Chinese crew. He, however, requested my interference in removing them from the vessel this morning, as he had heard they were not likely to fall into his views, but, on the contrary, to assist these very persons in carrying out their diabolical design and becoming participators in the plunder. The captain was afraid to return to the vessel; and I allowed him to remain on board till the evening, when he went off to Hong-Kong by the 6 P.M. steamer. The lorcha remains close to us."

A little trip to Canton in the "whale-boat" gave him another glimpse into Chinese life. "Walking on shore this morning," he writes, "I discovered the body of a Chinaman. He had not been long dead. He presented a most emaciated appearance, as if he had been starved to death. I asked some Chinese to remove the body; but they would have nothing to do with it, unless I paid them something." And, the next day:—"Walking on shore this evening, I saw a Chinaman burying the body I discovered yesterday. He just laid it under the surface of the ground, the mound barely covering it."

On further trial, the vessel was found to be such a wreck, that the Admiral referred to the authorities at home the question of her thorough repair or of "selling her for whatever she would bring." Meanwhile, the heat was so oppressive, and the cabins so close and contracted, that at last it became "hardly endurable." Bate, however, in spite of his self-accusings, was not a grumbler; nature and grace alike led him to look less at the cloud than at its silver lining; and so we have him adding:—"I often think, when I have grumbled at the weather or about anything else, what a pity it is I do not consider more what the effect would be upon me if matters were ten times worse. I would desire, in order to correct my habit of complaining, to look at the amount of misery and suffering around me, instead of dwelling on an ideal joy and happiness. A due consideration and contemplation of our present position cannot fail to call forth our earnest gratitude to God that He has made us what we are. For my own part, I may with truth say, 'The lines have fallen to me in pleasant places.'"

CHAPTER XI.

"'Cast thy bread upon the waters,'
Sow in faith the little seed;
Oft an unseen blessing hallows
Some unthought-of word or deed.
God shall give thee sweet rejoicing,
After many gloomy days;
And thine everlasting anthem
Shall declare the Master's praise."

THERE lay before him, during the succeeding year, a season of rough conflict. He was to reach his quiet haven, only after a stormy passage.

"A throne and crown await him,
Bought by his Surety's blood;
An endless rest in heaven,
A portion in his God."

And, meanwhile, to fit him to pass worthily onward to his home, he was enjoying an interval of quiet fellowship with more than one dear fellow-pilgrim.

"It was in the summer of 1856," writes a surviving friend in China, "that we became acquainted. It did not take long to learn to appreciate his lovely character—recommended at first sight to every one by the bright and holy expression of his countenance; which, like a sunbeam, shed light and joyousness upon all around him; and soon our acquaintance ripened into intimate friendship. Our Sundays, especially, were very happy days; for, after his own service on board ship, he often joined us at church, and spent the remaining hours of the day with us, when we enjoyed delightful converse. That beautiful verse of Keble's Evening Hymn seemed to me so applicable to him—

'When with dear friend sweet talk I hold,
And all the pleasures of life unfold,
Let not my heart within me burn,
Unless in all I THEE discern.'

Truly, with him this subject was ever uppermost. He loved to dwell upon the preciousness of our Saviour's promises, embracing them with childlike faith and simplicity, and striving to win others to enjoy that true happiness which those only know who love the Lord, as he did, in sincerity and truth."

In conversation, one day, he alluded to Hedley Vicars. "I have just," said he, "been reading his Memoir; and I am quite disgusted with the contrast of my own and of his character. What a noble fellow he was, and what a poor wretched specimen of a Christian man am I! Why, yesterday," he added, in a tone of deep abasement, "I went to the hospital to visit some of my sick men,—there was one lying very ill,—and, because one or two doctors were present, I actually had not courage to speak to that soul of JESUS!"

Another day, he said—"Oh! if you only knew what a lump of sin I carry about in my body, you would indeed pity me and pray for me. I have been thinking all this morning of that text, 'To me to live is Christ, and to die is gain.' Would that I could realise it every hour, every moment!"

In society, his constant aim was to "minister grace to the use of edifying." "In visiting ——," he wrote, on one occasion, to a friend, "mind you are not *led* insensibly into gossip. We often ourselves are entrapped, and only become aware of our imprisonment when we try to escape from it. Gossipping is an evil to which we are all addicted; and nothing mars the Christian character more, especially in ladies. Don't think, from this, I imagine *you* are a gossip: but we are weak and sinful creatures, influenced more by the smiles and frowns of the world than we are by our Saviour's precepts. Few Christian people are loved in this world except by their own brotherhood; but, when consistency marks their pilgrimage, they are always respected."

And he added:—"You will not, I know, think I am judging the people of ——. Far be it from me! I believe, if I were one, I should be the vilest. But you understand the power of money; and they are all there with the avowed purpose of gaining that power. I say, therefore, it is an atmosphere in which your moral health will not derive that benefit which I pray your physical health may. Seek that society alone, which recognises Christ as the Alpha and Omega."

"How few," it has been said,

> "There be among men who forget themselves for others!
> Verily the man is a marvel whom truth can write a friend."

"Many a person," writes another, "has said to me, 'Dear Captain Bate is such a true friend; he never hesitates to point out what he thinks wrong, and yet he does it in such a way that one cannot possibly take offence, but rather feels grateful; and then he so consistently himself perseveres in the right course, that one can't but listen to what he says.'"

Even on occasions where ordinary men shrink back into silence, his gentle influence, so mild yet so firm, few could resist. One day, he heard of a little difference which had arisen between two mutual friends. He went to the one in fault, and plainly pointed out to him that he had done wrong, and, by no harsh reproof, but by gentle persuasion, caused the friend to see his error, and produced union between the two. "So had he always," the same friend adds, "a word in season; and his good advice and connsel have been blest to many."

Another characteristic of his social converse is noted by Mr Irwin, thus:—"Unobtrusive in his religion and piety, he never would allow them to be assailed in his presence with impunity. On one occasion, a gentleman, who was sceptical as to the results of Missionary enterprise, boldly expressed his conviction that the professed converts were the worst classes of the population, and declared his doubts whether a single real convert had been made. Captain Bate felt indignant at such an assertion, and rejoined, 'You might just as well question the truth of the Acts of the Apostles, or the work of the apostles themselves.'"

Cowper says—

"As similarity of mind,
Or something not to be defined,
First fixes your attention;
So manners decent and polite,
The same we practised at first sight,
Must save it from declension."

"I remember," writes the friend already quoted, speaking of his delicate sensitiveness to the feelings of others, "during an argument in which he had become much excited and rather annoyed at some remarks that were made, he recollected that one lady present was an invalid; and immediately he went up to her and apologised for having in his excitement talked so loud and increased, as he feared, her headache. So very gentle," his friend adds, "and courteous was he always, and so ready to own himself in the wrong."

His warm heart was ever ready with its sympathies, even for the most unworthy. One evening, during a very severe storm of heavy rain, thunder, and lightning, whilst sitting in his cabin, he heard cries of distress. Immediately he rushed on deck; and a gleam of lightning shewed that it proceeded from two Chinese women, whose boat had upset, and who were being carried by the force of the current down the river. Instantly he gave orders for his boat to be lowered, and, himself proceeding to the rescue, succeeded in saving them from a watery grave. His kindness did not end there, but he took the poor creatures to his ship, fed and clothed them, and afterwards restored them to their homes.

The Lord Jesus, when He "dwelt amongst us," seems to have drawn to Himself the hearts of children. They were often about Him; for their keen instinct detected in Him a most gentle Friend. Bate possessed this beautiful characteristic to a degree quite remarkable. "He was wonderfully attached," says the friend in China already quoted, "to my dear baby, his god-child, and would nurse the little thing for hours, being as gentle and kind to her as a woman; and baby was always happy with him."

> "What happier recreation than a nurseling—
> "Its winning ways, its prattling tongue, its innocence and mirth?"

On his last visit to that mother, an incident occurred which she records thus:—"I well remember how that day he missed my baby, and had her brought to him. Afterwards, whenever I offered to take her, he would say, 'Oh! let me keep her; it is my last day here.' And she was happy in his arms for hours."

No surer test anywhere of a man's real nature!—

> "There is an atmosphere of happiness floating round that man,
> Love is throned upon his heart."

A child discerns it in a moment; and its decision admits of no reversal.

And it was not only an infant that attracted him. The child grew in years, not to outgrow his kindly sympathies, but to find in him a loving and condescending friend.

> "The friendship of a child is the brightest gem set upon the circlet of society,
> A jewel worth a world of pains—a jewel seldom seen."

"His fondness for children," says Mr Irwin, "was quite singular. He noticed them—entered into all their little sports and ways—and never seemed more at home than when amusing them and making them happy." One of the most notable of all his war-trophies he gave as a present to a little boy.

CHAPTER XII.

> "I travell'd on, seeing the hill, where lay
> My expectation."

BATE was the very model of a British sailor. "I saw him," says a naval officer, "bring the Bittern into Hong-Kong one middle watch on a dark night, threading his way among the shipping, and anchoring her close off the dock-yard in a position where few men in broad daylight could so successfully have placed her,—and all without a whisper being heard."

The summer and autumn were spent in "cruising about the Canton River," partly to "protect British interests," and partly to "promote the health and discipline of the crew." For a mind of his temperament, the occupation was monotonous and dreary enough; but events were soon to occur of a kind to test the bravest heart and strongest arm. Meanwhile, we accompany him on his cruise, noting some occasional incidents.

One day, he landed at Canton, and took a walk into the neighbouring country. "Some of the Chinese," he says, "were preparing the land for sowing the rice.

I watched two men and three women at work for a long time this morning. They were over their ankles in mud, turning the ground over first with very broad wooden spades, like the Irish; then raking it; and, lastly, smoothing and levelling it by drawing over the surface breadth-ways a long plank, weighted with mud at one end, and pressed down by a man at the other. The seed, which had just commenced to germinate, was then strewed with the hand over the surface of the mud and water, and so left. Others, again, were transplanting the young paddy made into bundles like young leeks."

Another day he visited a scene of a different sort. "I went," he writes, "this afternoon to the 'Execution-ground,' accompanied by Messrs Johnson and Burney. There had been no decapitations this morning; and the ground was saturated with water from the recent rains. Took a rough sketch of the place, and measured its dimensions, which are as follows:—Whole length from gate to gate, in S.S.E. direction, 194 feet; width at the entrance, 18 feet; broadest part, 33 feet; narrowest part, at the southern extremity, 15 feet. 27,000 persons are said to have been put to death in this enclosure during the last year. The area of the ground on which these executions took place, excluding the passage at the north end, is equal to 173 of an acre, or $27\frac{68}{100}$ perches."

Another day, some weeks later, he visited this "field of blood," on occasion of an execution. He writes:— "I went to the Execution-ground at ten this morning, accompanied by Mr Johnson, Mr Gordon Newton, and Lieut. Chisholm of the Sybille, and witnessed, from the roof of the carpenter's shop there, the decapitation of upwards of eighty criminals; one unfortunate wretch was 'cut into a thousand pieces' at the 'cross.' A more revolting sight I never saw: there was neither dignity nor solemnity in the ceremony; and the extreme sentence of the law was carried out in their most ruffianly style."

As usual, the "habitations of cruelty" were found to be redolent with the incense of the grossest superstition. A scene in honour of an "oblation to the moon," he describes, on a subsequent occasion, thus: —"Pulled out on the river with Mr and Mrs Parkes. The boats and houses were all illuminated, and had a very striking appearance through the haze which hung on the river. The moon was nearly full; and, at the close of the festivities, these illuminations, fireworks, &c., are meant as an oblation to it. Every Chinaman on this occasion considers it to be his duty to hoist a light or lights, according to his means, at the highest part of his residence ashore or afloat."

One morning, as the men were bathing, one of them for a moment lost hold of the rope and sank. There were several others just beside him; but, as he "could not swim a stroke," his disappearance was too sudden for any of them to render assistance. "We sent the jolly-boat," Bate writes, "to seek for the body, and also offered a reward of twenty dollars to any Chinaman who should pick it up that night. The Chinese, stimulated by the offer of so large a reward, soon set to work, and, two hours after he had sunk, brought the corpse on board. There was not the slightest mark of violence on him; and from the placid look of his countenance and natural position of the hands and fingers, I should suppose he was insensible at the moment he disappeared." And, the next day, he adds:—"The Chinese did not bring the coffin on board till near four o'clock, instead of ten A.M. as they promised. It was plastered over with some black pigment. I believe the man intends charging four dollars for it. The corpse was placed on the dingy, and, towed by the cutter and followed by the pinnace and gig, left the ship for the burial-ground, just four-and-twenty hours after he had gone from it in perfect health to bathe. The ship was unusually quiet all the rest of the evening."

Like all brave men, he was an ardent lover of peace. "Thank God for peace!" he wrote, one day, on receiving the news from England of the conclusion of the Russian war. "We have not heard the conditions; but I have not the least doubt that under Lord Palmerston's auspices they will be such as will be deemed honourable to all parties. Nevertheless, we feel our pride has been *a little* humbled. It will do us no harm; for there was far too much of the spirit —'By the strength of my arm have I done it; and by my wisdom, for I am prudent.' The difference betwixt a peace-establishment and that of twenty-two months of war has cost the country £43,564,000!!!"

A week or two afterwards, he writes:—"Rain! rain!

rain! without cessation the whole day. Business was carried on from house to house in boats and in chairs." And, the following day:—"The forenoon was tolerably fine; but in the afternoon the rain came down as hard as ever. Several houses have fallen down inside the city walls; and I hear that eight persons were buried in the ruins of one of them. Rice has gone up considerably in price; and I fear there is much distress throughout the country."

On August 7 (1856), we find him addressing a friend in England thus:—"I begin to think now that this will be the last time I shall write from China; for the next mail will bring tidings of our fate. I suppose we shall be all ordered home in the Winchester, and the vessel be sold for what she will fetch out here. I regret not to have the opportunity of bringing her home; for she is a beautiful brig, and in very good man-of-war order. My friend Captain Parker leaves by this mail for England, and I send the floss-silk by him. I have been at Canton the last week; but, owing to the long continuance of very, very wet weather, have been unable to move about there much. The whole place at high-tide is inundated; and, to go from one house to another, a boat is necessary. We had to embark at the first flat, immediately outside the Consulate-verandah. It was most absurd to see me going shopping for the silk. I entered the shop door in a sun-pan; and, while the Chinaman who served me was up to his middle in water, I was seated on the counter with my feet upon two high stools. For two whole months we have had nothing but pouring rain. The rain-gauge for the last month, July, shewed fifty-two inches. They say they have not had so much wet for years and years. Everything on board the Bittern is saturated with damp. I fear there is much distress in store for the poor Chinese. The rice-crops have been beaten down with wind and rain, and now lie rotting on the ground. Trade is almost at a stand-still here from the unsettled state of the country. I have this instant heard that all the crops have failed from *drought*. Is not this strange? The Admiral, Sir M. Seymour, is still in the north. We all take to him very much. He is a straightforward, honest man, and, I believe, knows his work thoroughly. I was away last night in my gig after pirates, and did not get on board till three this morning."

Another day, he writes:—"Moored off Canton, *August* 14. Performed divine service on board, and then attended church on shore. Mr Gray is an extempore preacher; very fluent and energetic; doctrine sound—full of Christ. In the afternoon, the congregation was very small. Five persons were present at the evening sermon, which commenced at five to-day. This is very discouraging to Mr Gray, who, I believe, does all in his power to bring them under the sweet influences of the gospel."

"A man is known," it has been said, "by the company he keeps." Bate never was on shore at any place without at once seeking out the missionaries. "Visited," he writes, one day, "Dr Parker's Chinese hospital. An

American gentleman, Dr Carr, ministers to the patients in Dr Parker's absence. The establishment is open to receive the sick every day; and certain days are set apart for operations. This morning, a man about twenty-seven years of age was operated on for stone: the calculus extracted was as large as a good-sized chestnut. The patient was put into an anæsthetic state, and is now doing well. I saw a heart-rending case of dropsy in a poor woman; and several Chinese were operated on by a native practitioner for entropium. Ulcers, gun-shot wounds, and abscesses, were the principal diseases which came under treatment this morning. The hospital is very close, and, I regret to state, very dirty—so different from Dr Hobson's."

On another occasion, he writes:—"Visited Dr Hobson's hospital. It was opened by a native expounding a portion of Scripture and finishing with a short prayer. The patients then came in as fast as Dr Hobson could attend to them. The chief diseases which came under notice this morning were ulcers and tumours, and an incipient case of leprosy. I left Dr H. pursuing his labour of love at half-past eleven. The hall was then full of applicants for relief."

Each day seemed to open a fresh glimpse into the sanguinary disposition of the people. "Off Canton," one morning, he has this entry:—"Some of the dragon-boats on the river sent against the rebels have banners flying, with this inscription on them, 'Appointed by his Lordship the Governor-General to exterminate!' What La Pérouse says of the Chinese Government I believe to be true, that it is 'the most unjust, the most oppressive, and the most cowardly, in the world.'"

A brighter feature of Chinese life presented itself, another day, thus:—"The literary examinations are also going on now in the city. 5200 candidates have presented themselves for honours, out of whom about seventy-five will be selected. The examinations, which are exceedingly strict, and conducted in the most impartial manner, extend over a period of ten days. The degree to be taken on this occasion is Kiu-jin, corresponding to our 'Master of Arts.' The B.A. degree is called Suci-tein."

The heat continued to be most oppressive. "Intensely hot all night," he writes; "unable to sleep even on deck with cot hanging to boom." And, the day following:—"Night fearfully hot. Not a particle of rest to be had. Got up more fatigued than when I turned in." And, the day after:—"Night frightfully close: unable to catch a wink of sleep." And, the next:—"This was the warmest night, I think, I ever experienced. There was not a breath of wind throughout it; but at about five A.M. it suddenly became overcast, and a fresh breeze from the N.E. sprang up, which cooled the atmosphere, and at once relieved us of that dreadful feeling of oppression induced by the closeness of the night."

Another entry gives us a glimpse into the ship's discipline. On September 15, he writes:—"Went to night-quarters at midnight; all hands taken aback. The first gun was fired in one minute and thirty seconds from the time I gave the order. Fired three rounds, both broadsides; and afterwards three rounds from the port side; which was done in two minutes and forty seconds. The guns being secured, we manned and armed ship; first musket fired in one minute and twenty seconds from the time of giving the alarm."

On the same day, writing to his old messmate, he gives a little retrospect of his doings, thus:—"H.M.S. Bittern, off Canton.—My dearly-beloved old P——, I am quite ashamed of myself for not having written to you before; but don't you suppose, because I have not, that you and your dear wife are any the less frequent in my recollection. I have served our dear friend Hill in the same way. However, being a Christian man, I don't so much mind, because I know that both he and you will exercise charity, and bear patiently the faults of a brother. You see now how the 'old Adam' comes out in me. You will naturally say, 'That is just the reason he should not take advantage of it.' I must now stop these explanations and excuses, and tell you a little of what I have been about since I last wrote. I applied for a ship when the charts were finished, and had some hopes of being sent either to the Black Sea or to the Baltic; but it was willed otherwise, and I had to wait till near the termination of the war, when an appointment to the Mariner was offered me. At this I was, of course, much disgusted, and remonstrated, when another vacancy occurred by Vansittart's promotion out of this vessel, which was offered to me instead of the Mariner. As the Bittern had only a few months to run, I accepted her, and left by the overland on the 4th of February for Hong-Kong, taking Calver, my old servant, with me. I must tell you, by the by, that all chance of promotion for the Palawan Survey, for at least three years, was gone; but they have made a regulation in the H.O. that promotion shall go by *seniority*,—one to be given every year, a lieutenant and commander alternately. Being comparatively young, and with some of those old *home*-surveyors before me, I thought it best to cut the department, and get into the regular line, where, perhaps, in one day I might get what years of toil had failed to bring, or, at all events, when I brought her home, if not before, I felt they could not withhold my 'post' step. I took command in April at Hong-Kong, and had orders to proceed immediately to Whampoa to be docked, she having got on shore somewhere in the neighbourhood of Hai-tan. When in dock, we found the damage she had sustained to be so considerable, that the Admiral would not undertake to pay out £1700—the amount it would require to repair her—without referring to the Admiralty; so I had orders to take guns, stores, &c., on board, and lay in the river as 'guardo' until instructions should arrive from home. This, as you can imagine, was a terrible 'sell' for me. I did not bargain for so inactive a life as that of lying at Whampoa, and with little or nothing to do but think of the intensity of the heat, the continual pouring of the rain, the irritation caused by the biting of the mosquitoes, and the entire absence of society.

"I, however, broke the monotony," he continues, "and absorbed a little of the time by getting under weigh, and taking a cruise down as far as the entrance of the river; and, before we returned, we were well into the month of June. I then remained a little time in Blenheim Reach, walking all over Dane's Island every day, and, after thoroughly exhausting everything of interest to me, came up here for a change; and a very agreeable change we find it, for there is a nice reading-room to go to, and we see a little of social life into the bargain. I like this man-of-war work better than surveying. I am now quite a gentleman, with little or nothing to do but look after my *yacht;* for a yacht the Bittern really is. She is in beautiful order; and I don't think a ship on the station would touch her, either in gunnery or aloft. We have an excellent ship's company, and are all very comfortable. I went to night-quarters the other night. Not a soul, even the first lieutenant, knew a word about it; and in one minute thirty seconds from my coming on deck, and bellowing out, suddenly, 'Quarters—action on both sides!' the first gun was fired; and three rounds were fired in two minutes thirty seconds. I am expecting the mail now every day, which will decide our fate. I fear poor briggy will be sold, and the crew ordered home in the first man-of-war. This will suit me, as I made arrangements to be in England in about a year from the time I left. However, man's plans are often set at nought; and I feel it wrong to say, *I* have made arrangements, &c. I sought God's guidance in my appointment to this vessel, and I am quite content to leave all to Him. This getting on shore may appear a great drawback; but who can tell that it may not ultimately turn out for my good? I believe it will."

And he adds:—"I shall now revert to something a little more interesting. I am ashamed to find that I have taken up so much of my paper all *about self.* How are you, my dear fellow, and your good wife and family? I asked you, in my last letter, to tell me *honestly* what I could send to my little godson which would be really useful; but you never answered me. I shall turn round upon you and make it a grievance, not having heard. If the Bittern be ordered home, what would I not give to bring her down where you are on my way? I wonder, my dear P——, if I ever shall have the pleasure of making your dear wife's acquaintance. It matters little, after all, whether I do or not here below. I do pray, however, that by God's grace we *shall* dwell together hereafter."

Henry Martyn once asked himself, "How shall I hold heaven constantly in view?" Often, very often, did Bate, during these months, urge upon his conscience the same weighty inquiry. And the answer we have in such records as the following:—"Performed divine service on board, and afterwards went to church on shore. Received the sacrament—the first time since leaving England. Remained on board the whole day afterwards, studying *Prophecy.*" Such studies constantly occupied his mind; and he found them eminently conducive to holiness and to growth in grace. Ever since he read the Scriptures for himself, he had been struck with the prominence given to the Church's "blessed hope;" and it taught him to "wait for the Son from heaven" with a very simple and lively faith.

"Oh for a well-tuned harp!" an old confessor used to cry, in some of his last and lonely hours. Bate also was unconsciously nearing the heavenly rest; and, as if already breathing its serene air, he would take up his ditty and say—

"For ever with the Lord!
Amen, so let it be:
Life from the dead is in that word,
'Tis immortality.

"Here in the body pent,
Absent from Him I roam,
Yet nightly pitch my moving tent
A day's march nearer home.

"My Father's house on high,
Home of my soul, how near
At times to faith's transpiercing eye
Thy golden gates appear!

"My thirsty spirit faints
To reach the land I love,
The bright inheritance of saints,
Jerusalem above."

CHAPTER XIII.

"Go labour on! 'tis not for nought;
All earthly loss is heavenly gain!
Men heed thee not, men praise thee not;
The MASTER praises! what are men?"

HAVELOCK a subaltern for three-and-twenty long years! Bate, likewise, was still doomed to the "shady side" of official neglect.

Before leaving England, he had quitted the Surveying-department to work out his promotion in the regular service; and, on this understanding, he had accepted the insignificant command now held by him. What, then, was his chagrin, to learn, by a private letter that autumn, that, scarcely had his back been turned and he was now out of reach on a distant station, when the Admiralty, still withholding his justly earned promotion, had ostracised him by ordering him for four dreary years to the inhospitable coasts of Tartary? "The Bittern, I hear," he writes, "is to be sold, and her crew sent home; and Sir C. Wood has requested the Admiral to bear me on the flag-ship's books until he sends out a steamer to enable me to proceed to Tartary on a Survey. This is too bad; unless he sends my post-commission with her. I was in hopes I had washed my hands clear of the *H.O.* This the Hydrographer knows; and it is hard to force me into the service again, unless the appointment be accompanied by a Commission in recognition of my past services in it."

Henry Martyn, on one occasion, when smarting under a trying disappointment, wrote—"In prayer I had a most precious view of Christ as a Friend that sticketh closer than a brother." Bate, also, was not without the same refuge. "However, it is our duty," he characteristically adds, "to obey; and I must hope that it is all for the best, although it is hard to reconcile myself to it."

A month later, when the rumour had been finally confirmed by his nomination to H.M.S. Actæon, he again writes:—"I am sure you have heard of my great disappointment in finding myself 'hooked in' for a four years' cruise in these seas, without their Lordships ever consulting me whether I wished it or not. It has made me almost mad with vexation; and, indeed, did I not know that the Lord ruleth, I should be quite in despair.

O England, England! is it thus that thou recompensest thy bravest and noblest sons? Verily, it is well for thee, if thy "Gorgon-visage of neglect" do not turn their generous hearts into

"Hard, dead stone."

No misdeed so dishonours thy fair escutcheon as this checking and chilling of thy children.

> "It is a pang, keen only to the best, to be injured well-deserving,
> And slumbering Neglect is injury—'Could ye not watch one hour?'
> When God himself complain'd, it was that none regarded,
> And indifference bowed to the rebuke, Thou gavest me no kiss when I came in."

Awaiting the arrival of the Actæon, he cruised for some weeks longer in the Canton-waters.

One evening, as he was walking on shore, he encountered an incident which he records thus:—"Two Chinese men appeared to be dodging me over the hills." Doubtless, they were watching for an opportunity to waylay and murder him. It is one of the revolting features of Chinese life. Since that time, in the neighbourhood of Canton, an English surgeon, walking alone one day, was kidnapped and decapitated; and, in a few minutes, his headless corpse was hidden in an extemporised grave. And, some days afterwards, as two officers were sauntering along a quiet lane, they observed some "braves," with matchlocks and large knives, skulking behind, with the intention of killing them: suddenly the strangers pulled out their revolvers, and the dastards precipitately fled; but, as the officers passed along, they came upon two graves, which some accomplices had dug in the road, obviously to receive their decapitated bodies.

Another of his entries is as follows:—"Performed

divine service on deck. Read to the ship's company one of Mr Melvill's Sermons (Gen. iii. 2, 3: 'The misrepresentations of Eve.') Immediately after our own service, I attended that of Mr Macey. He had a full congregation, and preached very effectively. He had an afternoon-service at five, at which there were about twenty-five persons, including two ladies." And, ten days later, he adds:—"Visited Mr Macey at the Bethel. He returned this morning from Canton, having been under medical treatment up there for the last five days. The illness is, no doubt, to be ascribed to his unremitting attention to a man who has for some time past been lying in a very precarious state from a bad disease in the worst possible form, and who died on the 5th instant. The atmosphere of the man's cabin was fetid to a degree."

Some days later, he says:—"Walked on shore in the evening. It was too hot to enjoy the walk over the hills. I felt quite tired after going over them. The heat prevents any rest at night, however tired you may *make* yourself in the day."

And again:—"Gathered a few Chinese names on shore this evening, while conversing with some Chinese. In the morning the captain of the Anglo-Saxon came on board to complain of his men being drunk and troublesome. Sent an officer and three marines to quell the riot. Communicated with Mr Vice-consul Bird verbally on the subject, and sent three of the worst of them to jail. The captain had his wife alongside in a boat, being compelled to resort thither owing to the indecent language the men were using."

One day he visited the Macao Roads. "Waited," he writes, "on the Governor, who is an officer in the Portuguese navy, and speaks English well. We then put up at Mr Duddell's Hotel; board and beds, three dollars per day. Bittern weighed, and anchored in 3½ fathoms off Macao at 3 P.M. Saluted the Portuguese flag with 21 guns, which was returned with the same number. The nature of the bottom off Macao is exceedingly soft, so that vessels may anchor safely in very little over their draught at low water. Some of the ships touch at low water."

Another day, when off Whampoa, he says:—"The English ship Hibernia anchored for tide about two miles below us. Mr Copeland, the master of her, sent on board for Whampoa mean-time. He had ascertained the error of his chronometer by our time-ball when at Whampoa, and was now about to put to sea without a rate but for the circumstance of falling in with us. We gave him Whampoa mean-time by ball at six o'clock. It is wonderful how indifferent some of the captains of merchant-ships are! putting to sea without a rate for their watches! a sea which, above all others, requires the most careful attention in navigating it."

Anchored off Canton, he writes:—"Performed divine service. Very warm under the awnings. Went on shore to church at the Factories. Mr Gray preached a very good sermon. Remained on shore at

Mr Parkes' until 5 P.M. service, and, after a stroll round the Gardens, came on board at 7."

The following day:—"The weather now is exceedingly hot. The northerly wind, blowing over the city, makes the Factories almost unbearable. They say September is the hottest month in the year from this very cause. Several Imperial junks, filled with soldiers, moving about the river. I imagine they are in attendance on the Viceroy, who left this the other day for Pekin. Nights very close and sultry. Mosquitoes on the increase. 92° in my cabin the greater part of the night."

And, three days after:—"Yesterday was the hottest day that has been registered at Whampoa for the last twelve years; and, as for this place, I think to-day is about the warmest which has been experienced for many summers. The temperature of the atmosphere so closely approximates that of the body, that the want of a cool medium to carry off the moisture from the latter is felt as most depressing. Feeling very unwell: this excessive heat causes great exhaustion and loss of natural strength. It completely prostrates me."

Five days later, he says:—"Exercised port-watch at quarters. They cleared for action and fired three rounds in 2¾ minutes. Numerous boats, full of Chinese troops, moving up the river into the Fatchan creek. There is a report that the Rebels are gaining ground in every direction. Rice is getting very scarce, and the price rising daily. The insurgents are only waiting for the rice-crops to ripen, to open the campaign."

At last, orders arrived to take the old craft to Hong-Kong to be broken up. On reaching it, he had a note from Dr Hobson:—"I am so sorry I did not know, in time, of your leaving the Canton-waters, as I should have liked to come on board and wish you good-bye. If I don't see you before you sail for Tartary (cold and dreary Tartary), I can only say, my best wishes will attend you. May your survey be speedily and successfully performed; your body and mind kept in health; and, above all, may your soul prosper and enjoy much of the Divine presence and blessing in your northerly expedition!"

Man proposes, but God disposes;—the sequel will shew—how.

"Mighty issues are impending, God alone can view the end;
But unceasing blessings follow those who find in Him their Friend."

CHAPTER XIV.

"We bid them listen quietly, as thankfully we tell
Of lives spent all unselfishly, of deeds of valour done."

"MUST make fight first!" was the brief but emphatic apophthegm in the mouth of the Chinaman, as sundry hints—more or less articulate—had recently reached him, of the foreigner's determination to open the gates of Canton, and to enjoy a more unrestricted trade.

Not many days before Bate quitted the Canton-waters, an incident had occurred, indicative of the hostile intent of the native authorities. "A lorcha," he writes, "anchored up here yesterday, and, in doing so, fouled a mandarin boat: whereupon they boarded the lorcha, and took one of the crew a prisoner until reparation, for the damage alleged to have been done in fouling, should be made. The owner of the lorcha complained to the consul; but, on finding that he had no clearance-ticket from Hong-Kong or sailing-letter, he refused to recognise her as a British vessel. I also cautioned him, that, if he came in sight of the Bittern having no colours or papers on board, I would seize him."

But a graver event followed. Early one morning in October (1856), as a lorcha (the Arrow), bearing the British flag, was lying quietly at anchor off Canton, she was boarded by a Chinese officer and a party of soldiers, who, notwithstanding the remonstrances of the master (an Englishman), seized twelve of her crew, bound and carried them away, and hauled down the union-jack. Instantly the outrage was brought to the notice of Yeh, the Imperial Commissioner, by her Majesty's consul, Mr Parkes,—who required that the twelve men should be returned by the same officer who had carried them off—that an apology should be made—and, further, that an assurance should be given that the British flag would in future be respected. After much higgling, the twelve prisoners were sent back; but not in the public manner demanded, and all appearance of an apology was pointedly evaded. The next step was to seize an imperial junk; but Yeh gave no sign of yielding. The two steam-frigates were ordered to Canton, to lie off the Factory; still without any result. And, at last, it was resolved—both as a display of power without the sacrifice of life, and as a proof of our determination to enforce redress—to seize the defences of the city of Canton,—"experience of the Chinese character (as the Admiral remarked justly in his despatch) having proved that moderation is considered by the officials only as an evidence of weakness."

Accordingly, the whole force proceeded towards the city,—capturing, on their way, several forts, including one (Macao Fort) which we shall revisit in the sequel, and described by the Admiral as "a very strong position on an island in the middle of the river, and mounting eighty-six guns." The Viceroy obstinately refusing reparation, a body of marines was landed to protect the Factory; the Dutch Folly—a fort with fifty guns, on a small island opposite the city—was taken; and another body of troops occupied the streets in the rear of the town.

Once more an appeal was made to the Governor, now with the additional demand that all foreigners should have the same free access to the native authorities and to the city as was enjoyed under treaty at the other four ports. Yeh replied by issuing, under his own seal, and by publicly placarding, a proclamation offering a reward of thirty dollars for the head of every Englishman. At the same time, nearly all the Chinese servants quitted the Factory. And nothing remained for our forces but a bombardment of the town.

Within the old city, surrounded by a high wall, was a large space of ground called the Yamun (or High Commissioner's Compound), and containing his Excellency's residence. Upon this a fire was opened, and steadily kept up from mid-day till sunset, another vessel shelling the native troops on the hills behind Gough's Fort in the rear of the city.

The inhabitants in the vicinity had been warned by our Admiral to remove their persons and their property; and during the whole of the succeeding night, they were busily engaged in this operation. The object now was to open a clear passage to the city-wall; and all the next day two 32-pounder guns, removed for the purpose from the Encounter to the Dutch Folly, maintained a raking fire, till at length, towards evening, partly through the aid of the conflagration of a large mass of houses in the line of attack, the wall opened to their view.

That night, amidst the stillness, an officer sallied forth from the flag-ship to reconnoitre. The Chinese were prowling about in every direction; but the stranger, with his life in his hand, quietly surveyed the position, and returned at daybreak to report "the practicability of a breach." It was Commander Bate, who had been placed on the books of the flag-ship until the Actæon should arrive from England.

In the course of the morning, a storming party was formed; and Bate volunteered to lead it in person. In the interval, as he stood on the bridge of H.M.S. Barracouta, surveying the position and placing the ships, a grape-shot smashed his glass and slightly wounded his hand. But, nothing daunted, he put himself at the head of the attacking party—mounted the breach—seized a Chinaman's flag—waved it with a cheer—and in a few moments the whole party was on the parapet in possession of the wall. The parapet bristled with loaded guns; but the "braves" fled—the gate was blown to pieces by a couple of charges of gunpowder—the main body of the assailants entered—and the day was ended by a visit of inspection by the Admiral to "the house and premises of the High

Commissioner," the whole force retiring at sunset, and the object of the assault, which was to convince Yeh that they had power to enter the city, having been fully accomplished.

"The way," writes the Admiral in his official despatch, "was most gallantly shewn by Commander Bate, whom I observed alone waving an ensign on the top of the breach."

The Colonial Chaplain of Hong-Kong, the Rev. J. Irwin, referring to the same scene, writes:—"I went up to Canton at the time of the first bombardment of the city and of the entrance into the Yamun. All had done their duty gallantly; but Captain Bate was singled out as most conspicuous for his coolness and bravery. One officer said to me, 'The sight left my eyes, when I saw Captain Bate standing alone on the breach amidst a shower of balls and a cloud of dust.' The only other officer or man who came up for some time was Mr Johnson, late Master of the Bittern. It was not rashness which placed him in this exposed situation; but he knew the locality better than the other officers, and so got the start of them." And Mr Irwin adds:—"His great coolness and self-possession in danger were frequently remarked. From his wonderful escapes, both on this occasion, and in leading the Barracouta when the spy-glass which he held in his hand was shattered by a grape-shot, it was said, 'The bullet was not cast which would kill Bate.'"

And another friend, also then resident in China, writes, in allusion to this occasion, thus:—"Our beloved Captain Bate's Christian graces now shone brighter and brighter, and proved to the world that the best men are indeed the bravest. He never flinched in any moment of danger; for he knew upon whom his hope was set, and dreaded not any evil."

Still Yeh did not yield. "The city of Canton," wrote the Admiral to him, "is at my mercy. You have it in your power to terminate a state of affairs so likely to lead to the most serious calamities. The deliberation with which I have so far proceeded must have satisfied you of my reluctance to visit the consequences of your acts upon the inhabitants of Canton. But should you persist in your present policy, you will be responsible for the result, and will learn, when too late, that we have the power to execute what we undertake." The only rejoinder was an offensive evasion, charging the "barbarians" with the blame of the rupture, and carefully avoiding the subject of their demands.

The fire was re-opened from a 68-pounder mounted in the Dutch Folly, being principally directed at a fortification crowning a hill in the rear of the city, hitherto considered impregnable; and, although at extreme range, several shells burst within the works, "the effects of which," says the Admiral, "must have undeceived the authorities as to their supposed security in that position." Another day, a fleet of three-and-twenty war-junks, collected under the guns of the French Folly, were attacked and demolished,—Bate with his accustomed skill and bravery leading the ships through the narrow channel in the face of a battery of one hundred and fifty guns. The fort itself was taken, after "an animated fire sustained by the Chinese with great spirit for at least thirty-five minutes."

The next step was to take possession of the Bogue Forts. The Admiral sent a summons to the chief mandarin to deliver them up "until the Viceroy's conduct could be submitted to the Emperor." "No," replied the mandarin, on the expiry of an hour, "I cannot: I should lose my head; and I must therefore fight." The forts were fully manned, having upwards of two hundred mounted guns; and the troops stood to them for an hour, till the enemy entered the embrasures. At that moment, the mandarins made their escape in boats waiting to receive them, their unfortunate followers rushing into the water until they were assured of their safety by the efforts made to save them.

A few days later, the capture of another series of forts, "on the opposite side of the Bogue entrance, and mounting two hundred and ten guns," completed the operations. And the command of the river was now in the "barbarians'" hands.

Might not the population of the city (it was thought) begin to feel the inconvenience of such an occupation of their River, and coerce the Governor into submission?

The Admiral had mistaken his man. A week or two passed; and Yeh issued another proclamation. "Since I have taken charge of my office," said he, addressing the soldiers and people, "you have looked upon me as your father, and I have looked upon you as my children. Four years ago, the rebels arose in several hundreds of thousands, and you ventured with united strength to resist them, which was very meritorious, not leaving a fragment of their remains. Now they have again raised disturbances, attacking our heavenly dynasty, destroying forts, burning the ships, and making war on the city. The anxiety on this account has entered into my very bones and marrow; and your united wrath, too, has been aroused. Now I have received the Imperial commands 'firmly to hold and resolutely to fight and maintain the war from the public Treasury ;—to blockade the river and sea—and to sweep out every fragment.'"

It was determined to await the arrival of reinforcements from England.

Meanwhile, a secret project was on foot, to burn all the foreign factories. At last, one night, in the middle of December, a conflagration burst forth simultaneously at different points, aided by combustibles, fire-balls, and rockets, thrown from the suburbs. The fire commenced an hour before midnight; and, in spite of every effort to arrest it, it raged till every house was destroyed, except one, which was forthwith gutted by the Chinese. The boat-house and church, being detached from the factories, were untouched, and became the quarters of our force on shore.

In that "retreat" we shall have another glimpse of Bate, and of the movements of his inner life.

We conclude the chapter with an incident of this period, illustrative of that singular tenderness of heart which, brave as he was in action and firm in duty, he never failed to manifest.

It was after the cannonade of the Bogue Forts. The batteries had been silenced, and he was landing with a party to seize the place. As they proceeded, he halted for a moment, and charged them "not on any account to fire on the flying Chinese after they had evacuated the fort." Scarcely, however, had they entered, when one of our fellows fired; and the ball took effect on the face of a Chinaman, carrying off the nose and front part of the face. "I never," said he to a friend afterwards, "saw such a sight, as the poor creature stretched out his arms in an imploring attitude." "He assisted himself," writes the same friend, "to convey him for surgical assistance; but he was soon beyond the reach of human aid. 'I was strongly tempted,' he added, 'to cut down the fellow who thus wantonly took away life.'"

CHAPTER XV.

"Can there be solitude, my God, with Thee so near?
Can I, in Thy glad presence, know distress or fear?—
In joy or woe, in life or death, my prayer shall be,
My Shelter, Shepherd, King! I would be found in Thee."

BEFORE joining him for a moment in the "organ-loft," we obtain some secret glimpses of him during the events of the preceding weeks. These will now be understood in the light of the narrative recorded in the preceding chapter.

On November 14, writing from the "British Consulate, Canton," to a young friend at Hong-Kong, he says:—"When I returned, very late last night, with the Admiral from the taking of the Bogue Forts, my sleepy head was wound-up by reading your nice chatty letter. It was such a pleasure to get it; for I had had no news of any kind since Monday last, the day we sailed to take the forts. It *is* quite true that I had my glass cut in two and bent double by a shot whilst on the bridge of the Barracouta. I also received a slight contusion of the arm at the same time. Thank God, those poor missionaries are safe! How is Mr Y——?

You tell me, by the last report, he was still living. I have a *flag* for you, one of my 'trophies of war,' so I hope you will value it. I wish this affair was over; I am sick and tired of taking forts, and seeing poor wretched Chinamen knocked over. We are very happy up here. The Chinese threaten us with an attack every night; and yesterday, in broad daylight, they tried to blow up the Niger."

Another day, he writes:—"Yesterday morning, we had a smart brush with some war-junks and a fort. I was on board the Barracouta, and never felt the shot flying about my ears so plentifully before. The Chinese made an effort last night to set fire to the ships, but, *of course*, failed. Poor creatures! I wish they would give in."

And again:—"I am just off to sink a large junk at the entrance of a creek, from which they have been annoying us with fire-rafts or gun-boats."

One day he was visited by a friend from Hong-Kong, the Colonial Chaplain, who writes:—"When I saw him at Canton, he was just about to go down to Whampoa to attend the funeral of the marines who had fallen. All of them, I think, belonged to the Bittern. He was in tears, and said, 'It makes me sad to think that the loss has fallen on my poor fellows.'"

Himself alluding to this on the following day, he says:—"I went off to Whampoa yesterday to bury my poor gallant Bitterns, almost the only men who fell at the assault. Poor fellows!! after four years and a half's hard service, too!"

In the same letter, referring to a child of the family, he playfully adds:—"'Whip' Addie for me. Tell your aunt I will try and get a Tartar whip for her out of the Imperial Commissioner's house, instead of an English one which I promised her."

Some days later, he again writes from the "Consulate:"—"When I have five minutes to spare, I must take advantage of it to answer your welcome letter. On Thursday, we took the French Folly, with the loss, thank God, of only one killed, and two or three wounded. Some little casualties, however, occurred afterwards, whilst blowing up and demolishing the batteries. Tell —— I have a nice little matchlock for him, which I will send down the first good opportunity. I have also a rocket-arrow for him, as a specimen of a Chinese lethal weapon. The affair was very well done. The fort was in our possession at 7.15 A.M., and about noon it was no more.

"Poor Captain Cowper's accident," he continues, in the same letter, "was most melancholy!—was it not? It occurred the day before we took the fort. Poor fellow! he was all ready to embark the following morning with implements to blow up the French Folly. I pray God it may be sanctified to us all up here; and may we remember, that in the midst of life we are in death!

"In the French Folly," he proceeds, "we found a proclamation offering one hundred dollars for our heads, and something higher if taken alive. A *reality* has been given, I am sorry to say, to these proclamations by the murder of two of our men, who foolishly went into a village opposite Macao Fort, for the purpose of getting some vegetables. The rascals managed to get the head of the marine; the blue-jacket took to the water, and was drowned. The Barracouta floated down this morning, and is now burning the village."

And he adds:—"I am glad you achieved the trip to the top of Victoria Peak. I would give anything for a stretch up there. We get plenty of exercise here, but not exactly of the right kind. The weather is getting severe, and I must attribute this wretched scrawl to desperately cold fingers; I can hardly feel my pen. I hope to be at Hong-Kong shortly; I want to come down to see my gallant Bitterns off in the Winchester. We have now 'quiet nights in the trenches.' The Chinese keep us alive now and then by throwing rockets, and firing a gingall occasionally."

We now follow him to the "organ-loft." Writing to a friend in England, December 27, he says:—"The night the last mail started (this day fortnight), the Chinese burned us out of house and home, the only buildings not destroyed by their fire being the church and boat-house. All hands are living the best way they can. The Consul and I have taken up our quarters in the organ-loft of the church. The Admiral and suite are on board the Niger, so terribly crammed, that the captains have to sleep under a kind of canvas hurricane-house fitted up on deck; and the marines, small-arm men, and a company of the 59th Regiment, rough it out in the club-house, and under tents in the garden. We have entrenched ourselves just in the rear of the ruins of the factories, by throwing a line of defence across the centre of the gardens, taking in the church. We expect an attack to-night. God bless and watch over you all!

"P.S.—My old favourite Bible was burned, with several other books, when the Factories were destroyed. You must send me out one."

Two days later, he again writes to his friend at Hong-Kong, still dating from the "Organ-loft, in the Church at Canton:"—"I am quite alarmed to see the date of your welcome letter. Since the receipt of it, however, I have not been particularly well. I hurt my back jumping across a ditch once; and the cold getting at it whilst sleeping in the open air all night so completely floored me, that I was obliged to go for a cruise in the Barracouta. It is not all right yet: and I have a splitting headache into the bargain. I have been very busy," he adds, "making a plan of our position for the Admiral, to send home by this bi-monthly. We were all on the tiptoe of expectation last night for an attack. I wish I had a Victoria Peak—about twice its height—to run up every morning before breakfast. We are regularly imprisoned in this place; exercise is out of the question. The rats are very plentiful in the organ-loft here at night; and the cold wind howls through the church with the most dismal tone. I hope you all spent a merry Christmas; mine was not much so, as I was laid up with my back."

During the occupation of the mainland, he regularly conducted the worship of the troops. And, with

"A heart at leisure from itself,"

he found moments to spare even for distant sufferers. "My love to yourself and to dear ——," he wrote, at the close of the year, to a bereaved friend in England; "I wish you both, with all sincerity, the choicest of God's blessings on the coming year. All for the best, dear ——. It is a great change. A few years more, and it will appear as a tale that is told; and the chastisement will be seen, more strikingly than now, in all its merciful bearings, for God *has* a reason in thus dealing with you."

Before another year expired, he was himself to be with his Lord; and it seemed as if already he was breathing the air of the land of Beulah.

"The harbingers are come. See, see their mark!"

At the close of the letter just quoted, he adds:—"May the Lord direct me in all things!" Day by day, he leaned more simply and confidingly on HIM. Like the Hebrew warrior in one of his hours of solitariness, he could say—"O God, Thou art my God; early will I seek Thee: my soul thirsteth for Thee, my flesh longeth for Thee, in a dry and thirsty land where no water is; to see Thy power and Thy glory." And, like another lowly saint, also deeply tried, but through grace "more than conqueror:"—

"I love my God; but with no love of mine,
For I have none to give:

I love thee, Lord; but all the love is Thine,
For by Thy love I live."

And a new attractiveness seemed to gather on him, in the eyes of all his fellows. Some Christians there are, so uncouth, so perverse, so angular, that, the longer you know them, "the more arduous it is to love them." How Bate unconsciously drew other hearts to him, we may gather from the words of a brother-officer who was constantly with him in those closing months. "Thrice happy," says he, "those who belonged to him! I count it all honour, and am proud to feel, that I was in any way so nearly attached to him. I knew, by intimate intercourse in public and in private, the nobility of that mind, in which an unworthy thought or motive of action never dwelt. He faithfully reproved, when it was needed; but he was the truest and stanchest of friends. And I loved him with all my heart. The good officer; the thorough seaman; the perfect gentleman; the Christian; zealous in his profession; devoted to his country; worthiest in the social circle; the faithful and consistent disciple of his Saviour, whose light so shone before men, that men saw his good works, and glorified God in him! But the idiosyncrasy of his nature —that peculiar characteristic which so distinguished him from, and placed him above, his fellows—was the breadth and enlargement of his mind, which could not harbour a little thought in his own breast, nor be content to let one rest in the breast of another. And, doubtless, it was that charity," he adds, "which suffereth long and is kind, which vaunteth not itself, seeketh not her own, is not easily provoked, thinketh no evil, beareth all things, hopeth all things, believeth all things, endureth all things—that greatest of virtues, charity, which guided all his actions. God give me grace and ability to follow in his steps, if haply I may find a place near him before the throne!"

CHAPTER XVI

"King of glory, King of peace,
I will love Thee :
And, that love may never cease,
I will move Thee

"Seven whole days, not one in seven,
I will praise Thee :
In my heart, though not in heaven,
I can raise Thee."

We now enter on Bate's closing year; and it found him in his wonted pathway of self-denying duty.

"Ye are told of God's deep love : they that believe will love Him :
They that love Him will obey : and obedience hath its blessing."

Such was, more and more, the spring of Bate's daily life; and it made him happy and contented even in the hardest service. An example at once of his manly energy and of his generous self-sacrifice we are now to record.

The conflagration of the Factories had inspired the Chinese with fresh courage; and the decision of the Admiral to postpone all active measures of reprisal till the arrival of reinforcements from home had been construed into a proof of weakness and of fear. Accordingly, one night, a small postal steamer had been attacked betwixt Canton and the Bogue Forts by a large fleet of "Mandarin junks;" the pilot and one of the crew had been killed, and two others wounded; a lorcha which she was towing, laden with a rich cargo from the Canton warehouses, had been captured; and the steamer itself had narrowly escaped the same fate. Some days later, another postal steamer, while on her way from Canton, had been cut off by a party of natives, who were on board as passengers for Hong-Kong, but who proved to be emissaries of the Chinese Government, hired to perform the tragedy; all on board had been murdered, with the exception of some native passengers; and the vessel itself had then been run ashore and burnt. At Hong-Kong, too, a diabolical scheme had been concocted, to poison the foreign community by mixing their bread with arsenic, and had been defeated only by the largeness of the quantity of the poison, which immediately betrayed its presence. Attempts, moreover, of the most daring kind had been made, almost nightly, to blow up and burn our men-of-war. In short, it seemed as if Yeh's threat to "expel the barbarian" was about to be carried into successful execution. And so difficult a task did it appear for our force to maintain its position, that the Admiral, after burning the western suburbs of the city, at length had proposed to withdraw from the river.

A council of war was assembled; and there seemed no alternative but to retire. Bate was there; and, feeling strongly how unwise it would be to give the Chinese even the semblance of a victory, he volunteered to fortify and to hold the Macao Fort, at whatever personal risk and discomfort. The offer was accepted; and, whilst the Garden was evacuated, and the church and boat-house were immediately burnt by the Chinese, he received from the Admiral a force of three hundred men, and proceeded to the fort, resolved to keep open the river, despite any efforts of the Chinese to block it up.

The task was one demanding not a little both of energy and of patient endurance. A few days previous, whilst the Admiral still lay off Canton with several ships-of-war, an attempt had been made of the most resolute kind to gain possession of the fort. Towards midnight, and at "a dead low neap tide," when none of our vessels could encounter the "passage" so as to render any effective help, a large squadron of war-junks had suddenly approached below the battery; and so well planned was the attack, that, not until the flag-ship had been obliged to stand for some hours on the defensive, and the rise of the tide had warned the Chinese that they must retire into the shallows to avoid our fire, had the little garrison been relieved. But Bate was not daunted; and, therefore, though the withdrawal of the force from Canton left the fort "the advanced position," he boldly set his face to the enterprise, and, with a band of three hundred men, took up his post on the little island.

Our first glimpse of him in this "Patmos" is in a

letter to a friend in England, dated "February 12, 1857." "I am sure," says he, "you have heard all that is of interest concerning our movements in this quarter. Since we have been compelled to retire from immediately before Canton for want of an adequate force to attack and to keep open our exclusive line of river-communication, I have had the honour of commanding this our advanced and most important position. It is not a very luxurious one; for, besides being at times hard up for something to eat and drink, we are annoyed nearly every night watching, and in some instances repelling, the attacks which the Chinese make on the fort. You will hardly believe it when I tell you, that for *four* months I have not taken off my clothes to turn into bed; and the luxury of a pair of sheets is almost beyond my recollection."

The day following, he gives to the wife of the Consul some interesting details of his fort-life, thus:—"Macao Fort, or, Advanced Position before Canton, February 13, 1857. My dear Mrs Parkes, I would rather you charged me with being a great bore in inflicting another of my wretched scrawls upon you, than with that of ingratitude in neglecting to give you my warmest thanks for all your kindness. The Barracouta's arrival last Saturday night was most acceptable to our famishing garrison, and the comforts *you* kindly forwarded by her most truly so to myself. When writing for a few needles, I did not expect such a nice *useful* little housewife as that you made me. Sunday was the first day we had tasted meat for a long time;

and, although you know I do not care very much what I get in the eating line, I enjoyed the delicious mutton you sent me on that day most heartily, and drank both your good healths, to myself, after it. The Siamese coffee, of which Captain Rolland and myself enjoy a cup every morning, is excellent. I like you to tell me that our position here *must* be maintained; and you may depend upon it, with God's help, the command shall be obeyed. I complain that it is so seldom you see ladies interest themselves in these matters, involving as they do the happiness or the misery of a large portion of their fellow-creatures, that, when I do find one, it always gives me *good heart*. I send you a rough sketch of the interior of the 'Governor's' quarters, with references. I don't know whether you have my taste for these kind of sketches. We are all very happy up here, all sorts of sky-larking going on in the evening; and generally at nine or ten o'clock the Chinese excite a little interest by firing gingalls at us. Sometimes we deign to reply with a ten-inch shell from one of the mortars; but this, as a general rule, is too expensive, and so we deal with them with Miniè rifles only. The 59th, with the exception of thirty-five men and an officer (a volunteer to remain), return to protect *you*, as I find we can do with a less garrison. I wish you would come up and inspect our 'posts.' Do you recollect going the rounds one night at the Factories? Our mess is most absurd! an *Irish* officer of the 59th kindly undertakes to look after it. Since the Barracouta's arrival, the table has been groaning with viands, morning, noon, and night; no economy; and probably in a day or two we shall be half starved again. In the absence of a good will to climb, a game of quoits is our favourite amusement; also jumping, leap-frog, &c.

"We are now," he continues, "very busy throwing up an outwork, to receive another long 32-pounder. We shall, when it is finished, have three in position, besides two howitzers (12-pounders), all looking towards Canton. You know we are now left entirely to ourselves—no ship near us—which is an excellent thing, not only because it makes us keep a sharper look-out, but because it frees another vessel to attack these rascals lounging about the creeks on the river, and lessens the chance of their blocking us in—which causes much anxiety to our good old chief. When we were demolishing the church furniture the night before leaving the Factory-gardens, for the double purpose of feeding our watch-fires, and of not allowing it to fall into the hands of the Chinese, I saved the velvet off the pulpit for you, thinking you would like some relic of the place. I hope you have looked at my glass? Is it not a monument of God's mercy?"

And he adds:—"I *must* tell *you*, that I have established prayers every morning in the fort. Poor fellows! many of them know not God, and, I fear, care very little about religion; but, as God has promised that His Word shall not return to Him void, who knows but that a great blessing may be the result? I pray the Lord may take you under His special protection."

To the Consul he wrote by the same mail:—"Our dear Admiral was here for a long time yesterday. He told me of the Government having approved of your proceedings up to the 15th October. This I never for a moment doubted; and now they must and will approve all that has followed. Taking a retrospective view of everything, I see nothing to regret: no one step would I undo; and I congratulate you, my good fellow, on the prominent part you have taken throughout. We have everything to be thankful for, and much to encourage us to future exertion. Mr Yeh's nose will be brought to the grindstone yet. He perhaps is not aware what a big rod there is in pickle for him; and I would not mind giving the first dozen with it. The Admiral was much pleased with the attractions, &c., of the fort. I told him we were quite capable of taking care of ourselves, and wanted no ship near us. So Encounter is released, and another steamer is available to operate on the river and keep open our communications. There is no doubt, with God's help, we will hold on *now* till reinforcements arrive. We are very busy extending the earth-work of our 32-pounder (56 cwt.) one gun battery, to receive another of similar calibre on a traversing carriage, both pointing 'forward,' *i.e.*, to Canton. When this is finished, my heart will rejoice. I heard of the Imperial rescript; what childish rubbish, to be sure!

"On Saturday last," he proceeds, in the same letter, "I sent Captain Boyle with one hundred marines on a reconnoitring expedition. He fell in with the *enemy*, and, after a little skirmishing with them, brought his men off without a casualty. Wherever you go now, you are sure to fall in with some soldiers. They entertained us last night by firing a few gingall shot into the fort from the eastern side of the river, from the village where the marine was murdered; and, a few days ago, they made a most ridiculous attack—upon the fort, I suppose—from the hillock immediately over it. We condescended to give them a few 6-pounder shot in return for their noble exertions. The rascals attacked the fort again last night, firing several gingall shot at us. I wanted to try our ten-inch mortar, and availed myself of the opportunity thus afforded. A shell went through the roof of one of the houses, and burst inside, the crash of which we heard distinctly. *After this*, we turned in quietly for the night. I regard these attacks, if they are worthy of being dignified by the name, as the greatest possible benefit to the fort. It not only improves the men in their exercise, but it points out our deficiencies."

A week or two later, he writes to another friend, thus:—"We seldom get a night's rest, from the Chinese attacking us so frequently. From nine P.M. to half-past eleven, they are pretty sure to open fire on the fort from positions on either side of the river, taken up sometimes inland, at other times in row-boats at various distances, where our guns cannot tell with effect, for no country affords better shelter or greater facilities for carrying on operations against a fort situate as this is, than that immediately around us. Thanks, however, to a merciful Providence and to good mud-walls, they have only succeeded in killing three of our men as yet; and as for capturing the fort, I will, *with God's help* (the italics are Captain Bate's), hold it against all China. The Chinese are a most contemptible enemy, as long *only* as we are active; but immediately we *cease*, they commence with their mode of warfare, which is illustrated in their burning of the Factories, in the 'Queen' and 'Thistle' tragedies, in the atrocious poisoning case, and in their recent acts of assassination and of cutting off unarmed parties; besides burning and blowing up all they can get at. In fact, it is a subtle enemy we have to deal with—an enemy whose cowardice in the field is only equalled by the abominable atrocities they commit out of it. We are anxiously waiting for reinforcements, to enable us to advance against Canton. Delays are dangerous. We must attack in good earnest, less as a measure of retaliation than of defence; for if we do not attack them, they will attack us. I have rather a heterogeneous kind of garrison under my command, consisting of sailors, marines, and part of the 59th Regiment, making a total of about three hundred men. It is the advanced position; and having no ships to support us, we are liable to be assailed on all sides."

To his friend Captain Collinson, R.N., he communicates certain authentic details respecting the resolution to occupy the fort, which reveal some characteristic features of the man:—"Advanced Position before Canton, Macao Fort, March 6, 1857. My dear Collinson, Very many thanks for your letter of the 2d January, and the kind congratulations from all your party, especially those of your dear mother, with her nice little note. I send her in return—which, when she has finished with it, she can hand over to *the* Association—a sketch of the interior of the room in which I am now writing. It is a small house, about nine feet square on the battlement immediately over the gateway—a kind of look-out house, which you know full well are always to be seen over the entrance of their forts. It is rather an exposed position; but it commands a good view of what is going on, and you have the advantage of being always at hand. In fact, it is the best house for the *Governor*, although perhaps the worst in the fort for comfort. I am sorry to say we have been obliged to retire from before Canton—*i. e.*, give up the Dutch Fort and Factory-gardens. This was a measure, of course, we all regretted; but it was one of expediency, and indeed necessary, on account of not having a sufficient number of ships to keep open our extensive line of River-communication—threatened, as it was, to be blocked up in four places. We were also menaced in several parts of our line by formidable flotillas, each division amounting to upwards of one hundred junks, besides row-boats—such a force as we never saw in the last war: and, what was more embarrassing, Hong-Kong was threatened, and the community turned immediately to the Admiral for naval protection.

"The Admiral, accordingly," he continues, "before

quitting the Factories, determined on a retrograde movement as far as the Bogue Forts—a measure in which he received the unanimous support of the Commodore and Captains (whom he admitted to his council), with the exception of myself. They recommended it on the grounds that it was impossible to guard so many points in the river, each of which could not be left without two vessels, on account of the daily increasing flotillas under organisation, and that some dark night we should find a portion of our squadron blocked in; that by retiring as far as the Bogue, all these vessels would be available to hunt up the enemy, and in the event (as was anticipated) of difficulties arising at our northern ports, we were in a position to give them support. Against this array of rank and opinion, I, a solitary Commander, urged the Admiral to *hold on* at all hazards, on the ground that if we once abandoned the river, the Chinese would be so elated at having *driven* the barbarians out, that the immense resources they have at their command would immediately be put into requisition to keep us so (and we know too well how effectually they can 'block up'), that not a vessel of any draught would be able to approach within fifteen or twenty miles of Canton. Thus the force which the Government send out to act against the city will be absorbed (especially in the summer months) before they get a glimpse of the walls of it. And with respect to our *worst* apprehensions for the safety of our Colony and Northern Ports, the very fact of our being beaten here would precipitate the crisis elsewhere—

that, in fact, our *holding on before Canton* is the *safest guarantee* for peace at the other ports. The Admiral *quite agreed with me;* but still he was so painfully anxious about the safety of his ships, and the possible contingency of being blocked in before twenty-four hours elapsed, that we made what would have been a most undignified retreat, had we not been obliged to stop at this fort to embark the garrison, &c. I was living on board the Niger with the Admiral; and at breakfast (while the boats were on shore getting the guns off, and Cochrane had just sent a message to say that everything would be off and the fort vacated by ten that morning) the Admiral put the oft-repeated question to me, knowing that I differed from all the others —'What do you think?' I replied that I was still of the same opinion, and that I would only be too happy to hold the fort till reinforcements arrived from England. Fowler, the Flag-lieutenant, who supported my counsel from first to last, urged him to adopt it—'at all events,' he said, 'till you hear again, sir, from Hong-Kong.' Happily, at this juncture, the Barracouta was reported *from Hong-Kong.* The Admiral immediately countermanded the order to evacuate—much to poor Cochrane's disgust, who had been all the morning hard at work getting the guns, &c., down to the boats—threw in a garrison of three hundred men, and honoured me with the command; and here he has kept me ever since."

And he proceeds:—"Hong-Kong is flourishing. The river, and ships guarding it, are intact. Our northern ports are in a state of perfect quiescence. Reinforcements have begun to arrive; and the General Commanding-in-chief has only to come to Macao Fort, and he is within half-an-hour's pull of the city of Canton. This may appear to you a little egotistical; but it is a plain statement of facts, and that is why I have told you. Now, do, pray, let me know whether you think my advice was good. I can assure you I felt a deep responsibility in giving it, standing alone against the opinions of all the other Captains, and at a time when affairs, I must confess, looked anything but prosperous. Being left now entirely to ourselves, my attention has been occupied in strengthening the defences of the fort. We mount seven 56-cwt. long 32-pounders, besides howitzers and field-pieces and a ten-and-an-eighth-inch mortar. The Chinese are constantly firing into the fort; and for the last three nights we have been kept up till midnight, replying to their fire. They generally commence about nine or half-past nine, by firing round-shot, gingalls, and rockets, from positions taken up in the creeks or well inland on either side of the river, affording good shelter from our guns. Last night, they concentrated far heavier fire on the fort than I have yet seen; but, thanks to a kind Providence and our good mud-walls, beyond opening a little daylight into the roofs of our huts, knocking a sentinel's cap off his head, slightly wounding the Captain of Marines, and grazing one or two others, no damage was done. I always hold our fire, in the hope of inducing their row-boats to approach nearer; for it is a hundred chances to one that you hit them, dispersed over so large a tract of country, and with the shelter which *you* know Chinese ground is so capable of affording. Their rockets are formidable, and very different from those in use last war. These go clean through the roof of a house; and one penetrated six inches in the Encounter's side. I wish you could see us in one of these attacks. I can only compare it to the battles in Rochester Gardens—the shot whizzing about one's ears. It is very exciting; and their guns make a terrible noise in a calm, dark night. Sometimes they commence at two in the morning; and just at day-dawn is a favourite time to fire a salvo and cut. What with the practice I had on board the Bittern, and the intimate acquaintance I have made with these splendid 56-cwt. long 32-pounders, and my attachment to the ten-inch mortar, I quite *look down* on a theodolite. It is not about angles you must talk to me now . my pets are fuzees, bursters, range-boards, &c.; and if I want to soar into the more intellectual part of it, the favourite toy is $x = \frac{\sqrt{3 \times r.}\ z.}{4}$; where r equals the range in yards, and . z the amount of fuze composition consumed in one second. In fact, the old Actæon had better keep away, unless she have some 56-cwt. 9 ft. 6 in. 32-pounders on board. I rejoice to see she only sailed on the 18th of December from Madeira; so that it will be good two months yet, I hope, before I am compelled to labour for that nasty H.O.

"I saw your letter," he adds, "in the *Times*. It is

shameful that another expedition is not sent out, now that the limits are so clearly circumscribed. *March* 10.—The Admiral came up yesterday, and inspected the fort at quarters. He expressed himself *so* pleased, and paid me the highest compliment I ever received from any commander-in chief;—*thanking* me, also, for all I have done. This is gratifying. God bless you all; and, with much love to all your home-circle, ever, my dear friend, affectionately yours, W. T. BATE."

The occupation continued to entail upon him the most harassing and exhausting labours. "These wretched Chinese," he writes to a friend in Hong-Kong, "try to annoy us nearly every night by firing gingalls at the fort. Last night, at about ten o'clock, I was walking up and down the parapet, grumbling to myself first about the Actæon, and then at not hearing from one of the inmates of St Paul's, when whiz came a gingall-ball into the bank, not half-a-dozen yards from me; and then a desultory fire was kept up for about three-quarters of an hour afterwards. We *did* condescend to take notice *this* time, because some of their shot fell very close; and we administered a correction out of an eight-inch mortar, which I imagine must have had a good deal of opium in its composition, as it had the effect of sending them to sleep for the remainder of the night!"

In the same playful mood, he refers to another matter, thus:—"What makes Mr L—— think I am going to be married? Please tell him from me, there is no such good fortune in store. The Admiralty take care of that. No! I am afraid I am destined to be an old bachelor against my will, or, if I live to return home in the Actæon bald and gray-headed, will have to put up with some young lady of forty-five, with a shrivelled-up neck and long hatchet-features, who will insist on appropriating a certain article of my attire, and bully me most frightfully. If I could get home now, tell him, whilst only *half* my head is gray, I might stand *some* chance of securing peace and quietness in my old age. We are quite out of the pale of civilisation here,—not a ship near us; so, you must make allowances, if you see me like a painted savage when I return to Hong-Kong. I must put this to one side now, as I see no chance of sending it. 'Dieu vous bénisse!'"

Then, after an interval, he says:—"How time has slipped by! Look at the date of this!!! I might have consumed no end of your good cakes all this time. A report was current, some days ago, that the fort was to be attacked,—the truth of which we had the pleasure of realising both last night and the night before. The rascals commenced each night at half-past nine, by firing round-shot, gingalls, and rockets, from positions taken up either in the creeks or well inland on either side of the river, affording good shelter from our guns. Last night, they concentrated a heavier fire on the fort than I have seen yet, and kept it up two hours and a half. Shot and rockets were whizzing about in all directions: happily, however, beyond opening a little daylight into the roof of a house here and there, knocking a sentinel's cap off his head, and sending a rocket so close to the Captain of Marines, that the back-fire from it went *down his back inside his clothes*, scarifying the person a little; no particular damage was done, although there were two or three very narrow escapes. I always hold our fire as much as possible, in the hope of bringing their row-boats closer; besides, it makes them *too conceited*, if we return it often. My men play the game in daylight. I am satisfied now that the best weapon to fight these fellows with is a good broomstick. I suppose they will try it again to-night. No opportunity yet of sending to Hong-Kong; so I shall put this on one side for *another* week or ten days."

The day following, he writes:—"As usual, the Chinese gave us two hours' amusement last night. Their shot and rockets came flying about the fort in all directions; but, most providentially, not a soul was hurt. One man had a rocket through his trowsers. How we all escaped so well, a gracious Providence only knows. They fired uncommonly well; every shot either hit the fort, or passed in good direction right over it. I can't write any more to-day."

The next morning:—"No attack last night; but three shots were fired at the fort at daybreak. I had half a mind to try a *rat* for breakfast this morning. Very hungry and nothing to eat."

The Sunday passed; and, the day after, he writes: —"I received your welcome letters to-day; and truly delighted was I to hear such good accounts of ——.

My grumbling was all turned into praise. In the former part of this letter I told you I did not believe you had not written; and you see I was right. I hope to be able to get down soon, to be present at the christening of my little god-child. As to your going home, I shall believe it when I see you off in the steamer. For a wonder we had 'a quiet night in the trenches' last night,—not even a rocket discharged at us."

During the occupation, he conducted the worship of the garrison, and with great fervour and unction. "The dreary months," says a friend then in China, "which he passed in command of the fort—a position of difficulty and considerable danger—he turned into a time of improvement to himself and others. Instead of being discontented at the many privations to which he was exposed, he was always cheerful, and encouraging those around him to be so. He instituted daily prayer in the fort—a blessing which, though not at first appreciated, was the means of leading many to think more seriously, and had a most beneficial effect. Of the seed thus scattered none can tell how abundant may be the harvest."

One other glimpse presents itself, and one eminently characteristic. "My dearest little fellow," he writes to a youthful relative in England, "I am so pleased that you have got the multiplication-table *all off* and at your fingers' ends, and also with the very nice drawings you sent me, that I have preserved the flag which I captured on the walls of Canton as a present for you. It shall be sent home by the first favourable opportunity. The Chinese try every night to take this fort; but I think it will be a long time before they succeed, especially when we put all our strength in GOD, while they put theirs in stupid wooden dolls, which can neither see, hear, nor speak."

CHAPTER XVII.

"So I saw that despondency was death, and flung my burdens
from me,
And, lighten'd by that effort, I was raised above the world;
Yea, in the strangeness of my vision, I seem'd to soar on wings,
And the names they call'd my wings were Cheerfulness and
Wisdom."

THAT spring a gleam of sunshine fell upon his shady path. "Purity of motive," it has been said,

"And nobility of mind, shall rarely condescend
To prove its rights, and prate of wrongs, or evidence its worth to
others."

And calmly and steadily he had laboured on, not moved by man's neglect. But now it seemed as if the way was to be smoother and less rugged. "Most cordially do I congratulate you, my dear Bate," wrote Mr Parkes, the British Consul, alluding to the intelligence of his promotion to the rank of Captain in acknowledgment of his recent brilliant achievement in mounting the breach on the walls of Canton, "on the good news for yourself brought by this mail. You have got your post, I am told; and the value of it is, that it has been thoroughly deserved. I have not heard how it will affect you—whether the Surveying or Home is in prospect; but you will be guided as is best for you by One who will be near you, for you seek to find Him. Sir John, who has just come in, tells me to present his congratulations,—which, from whatever quarter they may come, will, you may depend upon it, be sincere."

The Consul's congratulations were only the key-note of the joy which pervaded the whole fleet. "This is to certify to Captain Bate, R.N.," was the characteristic round-robin which emanated from one little knot of friends, "that his health was this day drunk in Committee, and all further success wished to him by his very faithful friends, THOMAS WADE, W. WOODGATE, HARRY L. PARKES.

"P.S.—Hurrah for the right man in his right place. T. W."

Another friend, the captain of the flag-ship, wrote:—"No fellow feels more pleasure at congratulating you on your promotion than (no man deserves it more), yours, W. K. H." And another:—"Among the many congratulations you will receive, I feel sure that none are more sincere than mine. The only satisfactory intelligence received by this mail is the promotion of yourself, whom we all love and respect." And one other:—"Let me offer my most sincere congratulations that you are at last made Captain; and, though we all expected it, yet none the less pleasure does it give to see your claims thus acknowledged."

Bate lived for a nobler end than to court men's

praises; his one aim was to approve himself to his Master in heaven. Yet

"There is a blameless love of fame, springing from desire of justice,
When a man hath featly won and fairly claim'd his honours;
And then fame cometh as encouragement to the inward consciousness of merit,
Gladdening by the kindliness and thanks, wherewithal his labours are rewarded."

Bate was not a stoic; and he did not pretend to be indifferent either to the honour thus tardily awarded to him, or to the warm sympathy which it evoked from all around him. "The happy intelligence of my promotion," he wrote, from the Macao Fort, "has reached me by last mail. I say happy, because one feels thankful to get to the top of the tree, and take rest. My advancement now is certain; for I will get pushed upwards *nolens volens,* and no exertion on my part will either facilitate or retard me getting my 'Flag,' please God to spare me. And, moreover, I am, so to speak, independent of the Admiralty; no more begging and hunting up interest to get forward, or even to get what is justly due to you. Thank the Lord for His goodness! And I trust I should have thanked Him just the same, if He had thought fit to withhold it."

And, a few days later, to another friend:—"I am most thankful for your letter written on Christmas-day, conveying as it does the assurance of the interest you still take in me, and also the kind congratulations of all the dear ones around you. Most warmly and promptly do I respond to the prayer that you may all live, with God's blessing, to meet, not only next Christmas, but for many that are to come."

A poet writes,—

"How beautiful thy feet, and full of grace thy coming,
O better kind companion, that art well for either world!
His eyes are ray'd with peacefulness, and wisdom waiteth on his tongue;
Seek him out, cherish him well, walking in the halo of his influence:
For he shall be fragrance to thy soul, as a garden of sweet lilies."

Such was Bate among his fellows. "I certainly," writes the Colonial Chaplain, already quoted, "never knew any one who seemed to be such a general favourite. All classes and all grades spoke well of him. In his own profession, and amongst the military, there was the same estimate. I had the pleasure of knowing intimately many of all ranks in both professions, and never met one who did not speak of him in the very highest terms." This explains the rare cordiality with which his promotion was hailed throughout the whole force. Each one felt almost as if it were a personal honour to himself. We shall learn immediately how strikingly the same feeling shewed itself on an occasion greatly different.

What was the secret of this respectful affection which he enjoyed?

Bacon distinguishes two kinds of praise. "If it be from the common people," he says, "it is commonly false and naught, and rather followeth vain persons than virtuous; but if persons of quality and judgment concur, then it is (as the Scripture saith) 'like a fragrant perfume,'—it filleth all round about, and will not easily away." Bate's popularity was of this latter kind; and the source of it is indicated by his friend Mr Irwin thus:—"This general appreciation of him was, I think, owing not simply to his rare merit and worth, but to his still rarer manly, open-hearted character, and unaffected humility and unselfishness."

We note these things, not to glorify the man, but to point other eyes to the pattern of generous self-sacrifice which Bate exhibited so strikingly. Not every officer is gifted with his clear head, and firm hand, and eagle-eye; but who may not aim to follow him in that "strong-springed," lofty nobleness of motive and of aim which was graven, as with one of heaven's own sunbeams, upon his every action and his every word?

Week after week, amidst many hardships and privations, he continued to hold the fort. "Your letters," the Consul wrote to him one day, "were most truly welcome; and glad indeed were we to see that you are so well able to sustain yourself, both in cheerfulness and in strength, in your most trying and irksome position; and still more delighted were we to notice the hope you hold out to us that you may be able to obtain a short relief, and do us the great good which your presence among us, though for a very short space of time, would afford. I can well understand, however, that you would be slow to leave in the hands of any one the important position you hold, and which is not only the bulwark—I might say almost the sole one—of our present safety, but the key to all our future operations."

And another friend wrote:—"The pleasures of Macao Fort must now be exhausted, and I confess myself I should prefer my ship to your berth. If you can spare time to write a few lines, I should be very glad to know how you all fared the night they opened such a confounded fire upon you. I was then at Powder Island, and could count four or five flashes a minute."

Some further glimpses he himself gives us at intervals. Writing to Colonel Maclean, R.A., Commandant at Carshalton, he says:—"I was delighted to receive your letter of the 8th January, and sincerely do I thank you for your kind congratulations. Our dear old Admiral is a fine fellow, and glad was I to be of use to him in all the operations he felt it his duty to undertake against this obstinate Commissioner, Mr 'Yeh.' Since we were compelled to retire from immediately before Canton, I have had the honour of commanding this our advanced and most important position. I have rather a heterogeneous garrison, being composed of sailors, marines, and part of H.M. 59th Regiment, which at first amounted to three hundred men, but now only to two hundred and thirty. The Chinese taking advantage of our isolated position,—for we have no ships to support us, they being all employed in keeping open our extensive line of river-communication, which the Chinese have threatened to block up with stone-junks in one or two places,—we get attacked nearly every night. They open fire generally about nine o'clock, with guns in small row-boats, and with gingalls and rockets, from positions taken up on either side of the river in the creeks and behind the bunds and ridges of land, which, as you know full well, afford admirable shelter from our guns. If the night be dark, the rascals send up light-balls, and illumine the fort, for the row-boats to direct their fire. Providentially, we have only had three men hit, although their fire is admirable, not a shot missing. I always hold our fire, in the hope of bringing the boats out from their cover, and inducing them, if possible, to approach nearer; but this they are too wide-awake to do. We have now been so long inactive, that it gives them great pluck; for they put it down to this, that either we are afraid, or we have not power to attack."

And, in the same letter, he adds:—"I was greatly disgusted at being appointed to the Actæon without being even asked whether I liked it or not. I detest the Surveying-service, and, in taking command of the Bittern, was in hopes I had washed my hands clear of it. However, all is for the best. I was under the impression you had given up all idea of sending your boy into the navy, and that you had placed his name on the list for an artilleryman. You will get nothing out of P—— R——; but I admire his honesty in telling you, in the straightforward way he did, that he could not serve you—so *very* different from their Lordships' usual policy. I hear the Actæon is quite full. Things would have been different, had I been in England when she fitted out. I should like very much to have your boy with me, if you can make interest to get him into the service. Fishbourne, also, wants to get a nephew into the Actæon; but I fear there is considerable difficulty in getting boys into the navy, particularly as we are on the *reduction-tack*."

In another letter, in anticipation of a visit to Hong-Kong, he says:—"If I do come, you must promise not to make me keep watch; for a comfortable 'all night in' between a pair of clean sheets will be quite a novelty as well as a treat to me. I have not taken my clothes off to go to bed since I was last at Hong-Kong, just before the Factories were burnt. Tell —— I hope he keeps his pistol in better order now,—or the Chinese might storm the college, in his watch, with impunity. The cake you sent is particularly good in the middle of the day, and much more wholesome than the dust and dirt which abound in this domain of mine. I am delighted to hear the colony is quiet; and I trust, please God, it will continue so. Say to —— and ——, I shall be very glad if they will *honour* me with a visit at Macao Fort. I can't promise them much in the shape of luxuries. It really was very clever of little Addie. What a retentive memory the child must have! How is baby-boy? Now really I cannot write any more rubbish. I must go to ——.* I am so sleepy; and, just as one

* Here he inserts a hieroglyphic for a bed, in the shape of a transverse section of a series of planks laid in the most original fashion possible, and giving the idea of the utmost discomfort. For four or five months, he had no other.

is going off into a slumber, probably bang will go a gun, or fire will come a rocket! My house, which is nine feet square, is rather in an exposed position, being situate on the top of the battlement immediately over the gateway, the walls of which are one China-brick thick, and quite pervious to gingalls or rockets. When *you* come, however, I will put some sand-bags round it. God bless you! Good night."

And, to an afflicted friend in England, he writes:—"How mysterious are the ways of God in His dealings with either nations, families, or individuals! but may you and all who are in affliction take comfort from this, that a time is fast approaching when all that now seems dark and mysterious to us will be clear and bright! And with what wonder and gratitude shall we look back on all the dealings of a tender Father, who knew from the beginning what amount of discipline was necessary for us! So that we may join with the Psalmist in saying, 'Thou which hast shewed me great and sore troubles, shalt quicken me again, and shalt bring me up again from the depths of the earth,' and may 'forget our misery, and remember it as waters pass away.' But I fear I am irritating what I would fain soothe.

> 'Oh for a heart magnanimous to know
> Thy worth, poor world, and let thee go!'"

The relative to whom these solacing words were addressed, was himself quickly removed; and to his bereaved widow Bate wrote:—"Your own affectionate heart will tell you that I have no wish whatever to recall the painful incidents of the past, or in any way to be the cause of adding one pang to the anguish you have all suffered: yet I cannot allow this mail to leave without expressing my sincere and heartfelt sympathy in the deep affliction in which it has pleased an all-wise Providence to plunge you: and, although not feeling the loss as intensely as yourselves, believe me, the blow was, nevertheless, a very severe one; but never can *I* forget the fatherly care of that dear uncle whose death we now so much deplore. My prayer is, dearest aunt, that you have all received comfort from that *one source* whence alone it is to be drawn—even from HIM who *indeed* was sent to bind up the broken-hearted and to comfort *all* that mourn."

One other glimpse we have of him in the fort:—"We have not been able," he writes, "to take any walks yet; and now I fear I shall have to leave without doing so, as I expect the Coromandel over every hour, to drag me away from this charming place. The poor Raleigh is still hard and fast! I do hope she will be got off; but it is an herculean task." And he adds this postscript:—"I am afraid Mrs Parker will not allow me to take baby to the fort. Is it not a great shame of her?"

Events now occurred, which induced the Admiral to abandon a position which, for the last five months, had been maintained at so much hazard. And Bate, though deeply regretting the step—a regret which the subsequent operations amply justified—quitted a spot which, with all its perils and privations, had been lighted up into a bright sunshine, for himself and for others, by that "godliness with contentment," which, anywhere,

"Be the pillars of felicity."

An event had illustrated that dreary season, which, though little accounted of in human annals, is noted by the recording angel in heaven. "One instance I *know*," writes a friend then in China, referring to his missionary efforts among the men under his command, "of a soul being thus brought from darkness to light—to a saving knowledge of his Saviour." Memories like these will live, when all others have perished. In the archives of Eternity it is written, "This man was born there."

CHAPTER XVIII.

"Still, my Master, Thou requirest
Service here a little while;
Help me, then, to work with patience,
Cheer me by Thy love and smile."

It was the middle of summer, and the first reinforcements from England had already reached the Chinese waters, when all hearts were startled by the outbreak of the Indian revolt. "China can wait—India presses," was the spontaneous decision abroad and at home: the troops were ordered to Calcutta; and Yeh was respited for six months. At their close, Captain Bate was to "finish his course;" and meanwhile,

"He went zealously forward, God blessing his faith."

Scarcely had he quitted the Macao Fort, and repaired to Hong-Kong for a few weeks to recruit his health, which had begun to suffer from the incessant watching and protracted confinement, when he was suddenly summoned on a fresh errand.

In the brief interval spent at Hong-Kong, he had brightened by his heaven-lit presence a bereaved mourner's home. "In the hour of trial and of sorrow," writes the Colonial Chaplain, "I found him one of those whose friendship and sympathy were a solace. Little did I think, as he wept tears of affection and of grief over the remains of my beloved wife, and assisted with his own hands in depositing them in the grave, that so short a time would elapse ere he was himself to find a resting-place near hers, in the same hope of the resurrection to eternal life."

Like the Master, he had "the tongue of the learned" to "speak a word in season to him that was weary;" and his own joyous hope gave a peculiar edge to his words of tender sympathy. "I hope," he wrote, a few days afterwards to a member of the sorrowing family, "you experience that consolation which a firm trust in God, alone, can impart to His afflicted children. You have my prayers, poor and feeble as they are." These were not the hackneyed phrases of a withered, dead Phariseeism,—they were fresh, living distillations from the springing well of his full heart. His own departure was to be unheralded by any note of warning; and it seemed as if already he was unconsciously catching the symphonies of the place of rest and of joy.

"World of spirits! bright and lovely,
Where the wearied find their rest;
Where no sin, no danger enters,
Where no cruel foes molest.
Oh! it is not all such darkness;—
Beams of light break forth for me,
Once again my hope rekindles,
And I long to be set free."

One day, the Admiral remarked to Mr Irwin—

"Wherever duty is to be done, or difficulty or danger to be met, there your friend Captain Bate is to be found."* An emergency had just presented itself; and Sir M. Seymour despatched him to meet it.

"I am suddenly ordered off," he writes, in the letter last quoted, "to Singapore and the Straits of Banca, and am all in confusion. I leave in the Inflexible at four."

And, some days afterwards, "On board H.M.S. Inflexible on her way from Hong-Kong to Singapore," he writes, to a friend in England, thus:—"You doubtless will be surprised to see whence this is dated. The mail arrived last Wednesday, and brought intelligence that the Himalaya had been on shore—that the Transit was a total wreck in the Straits of Banca—and that the Actæon also had been on shore in that locality and knocked part of her main and nearly all of her false keel away. The Admiral despatched me, at three hours' notice, with orders to proceed to the wreck and see what could be done with the troops, stores, &c.; the former to be sent to Calcutta without delay. The Actæon and Dove had also been sent to the assistance of the Transit. We expect to arrive at Singapore the day after to-morrow, where probably I shall find my ship. When the affair of the Transit is over, I am to return to Hong-Kong to accompany the Admiral and Lord Elgin to the Gulf of Pechili

* In a letter to a relative, dated "Hong-Kong, July 10, 1857," he incidentally remarks—"To use the Admiral's own expression,—'I can't do without you, Bate:' but this *entre nous*."

in September. All this, of course, is contingent on Indian affairs, which at present look rather gloomy."

Two months later, from "H.M.S. Inflexible, one hundred miles from Hong-Kong," he writes:—"My last letter to you was written on board this vessel when about the same distance from Singapore as we are now from Hong-Kong. I was then on my way to join, as I supposed, the Actæon; but, much to my disappointment, I found that she had left for Hong-Kong just four days previously to my arrival. However, as I had business relative to the unfortunate Transit, I did not so much care about missing her, and proceeded immediately to Banca, the scene of the disaster. We arrived on the 2d August, and found the people encamped on shore in a bay, about a quarter of a mile from the wreck. The Transit was stiff in the position in which she first settled down after striking, her bows thirty feet out of water, and stern in nine fathoms,—in fact the very reverse of the picture the 'News' had of her some months ago. As I had full authority from the Admiral to act with regard to the disposal of the vessel in the way I considered most advisable, I at once made up my mind to put the old craft up to public auction just as she stood, with all the stores that were under water, everything having previously been recovered which could be got up. The vessel's back is broken; and the damage she has otherwise sustained does not make it worth any one's while to attempt to save her.

"I walked across the island by a jungle-path," he

continues, "to visit the Dutch authorities; and, as they have been so very kind to our shipwrecked people from first to last, I paid them a great compliment by requesting them to take charge of the wreck in our absence—as I had orders to bring all the people away—till she was sold or otherwise disposed of. They willingly accepted the charge; and, after making a survey of the place, we left on the 5th for Singapore, the poor Transit's people being right glad to exchange their gipsy-life in the jungle for the clean, wholesome deck of a man-of-war. We have lost one poor fellow from fever; and our upper deck is turned into an hospital, for the accommodation of several men, who, now that the excitement is over, tumble into the doctor's list at a rapid rate."

And he adds:—"I published a notice, which perhaps Mr 'Punch' will get hold of, that the vessel will be sold by public auction on the 10th of Sept.; and, whether the Admiralty approve of it or not, I believe it to be a providential thing she is lost; for all hands agree that she would have foundered at sea, in the next gale of wind she encountered."

Ten days later, he subjoins this postscript:—"*August* 28. On my arrival at Hong-Kong, I found my ship, the Actæon, in harbour; and I took the command on Friday, the 21st."

He must now have sailed for Tartary, to pass, upon its inhospitable shores, an exile of four years; but Canton was still to be taken, and Bate could not yet be spared. Accordingly, he was directed to cruise in the Chinese waters, until the operations against the city could be begun. Some occasional glimpses into his inner life in those months reveal a gradual ripening for the glory which he was so soon to enter.

One day, at Macao, during a fearful typhoon, hearing that a small brig had been disabled, and was in distress, he went out to her relief, and arrived just in time to prevent her becoming a prey to pirates who were hovering around her. "He seized the opportunity," writes a friend in China, already quoted, "to speak seriously to the master and mate of the ship, whom he heard swearing—pointed out how merciful God had been in delivering them from so great danger—and, after talking to them very earnestly about Christ, he knelt down and prayed with them."

Another day, in conversation, a friend remarked that the believer, though relying fully on God's promises, often forgot them at the right time, but that there was one precious truth on which the soul, however tempted, could cast itself, as on a sure resting-place, "Because I live, *ye* shall live also,"—adding, that, when fears and doubts oppressed, and the darkness was so thick that no ray of light could penetrate it, this promise of Christ was sufficient, and more than sufficient. "Yes," said Captain Bate, "it is quite true; but I prefer such a truth as 'Jehovah-jireh'—God all-sufficient; for, in the application of a particular promise, I am afraid that I may sometimes be mistaken, but in simply depending on God's all-sufficiency, I never can."

A week or two afterwards, in conversation with the same friend, he was deploring deeply his "evil heart of unbelief," his "body of sin and death," his shortcomings, and the slenderness of his attainments—"so far beneath what they might be consistently with his privileges and his experience." "But the Christian life," interposed his friend, "is a struggle—a race—a conflict; and, remember, that, if you are so continually harassed by sins of infirmity, the great apostle of the Gentiles was the same." "Yes," Bate replied, "we must through *much* tribulation enter the kingdom." And, after a few moments, he added:—"I am sure those are happiest, not who escape trials the most, but who are enabled to bear them the best."

On the same occasion, the conversation taking another turn, some one remarked, that Christ was Himself "made perfect through suffering"—that He "learned obedience by the things which He suffered"—that He himself took up a daily cross, and that we could not be exempted from it. "I have often wondered," said Bate, "why Christ should take up the daily cross, seeing He was already perfect. Was it, that those long nights of prayer so often recorded, that patient endurance of the contradiction of sinners against Himself, had the effect of raising the human element in Him beyond the glory of its original innocence and purity?"

And, another day, returning to the same subject, he said:—"It is indeed a great mystery—a depth which we cannot fathom; but don't you think, that, inasmuch as virtue tried and triumphant ranks far higher than innocence, it must have been necessary that Christ, if He was to possess our nature in its utmost perfection, should possess it in a state of victorious trial?"

Cowper writes—

"If His word once teach us—shoot a ray
Through all the heart's dark chambers, and reveal
Truths undiscern'd but by that holy light,
Then all is plain. Philosophy, baptized
In the pure fountain of eternal love,
Has eyes indeed."

Who does not feel, on reading those thoughts of Bate's, on a theme so transcendental, that he has been walking in God's own living light, and, in that light, "sees light"?

And it was not a barren dogma, but a felt reality, vividly graven on his heart by the finger of the Cross-bearer. Those tedious and weary hours, which he had passed so uncomplainingly, were spent at the feet of Him who "spake as never man spake." And who ever sat there in vain?—

"Thou teachest much by chastening
For old, besetting sin;
By pain, by want, by weakness,
By ceaseless discipline.
Thou teachest by temptations,
By weary vigils kept,
By deep and earnest conflicts,
By troubled slumbers slept."

CHAPTER XIX.

"Trust in God, to strengthen man;—be bold, for He doth help."

ONE Christmas-day, during the memorable defence of Jellalabad, the "illustrious garrison" was assembled on parade, when a well-known voice gave the word—"Let us pray!" It was Havelock, leading the army's thanksgivings to God, who "had in His mercy enabled them to complete the fortifications necessary for their protection." Bate, also, was not ashamed to be known to take everything to the feet of Jesus. "His judgment," writes an officer of the fleet, "was most accurate, as events always proved; and the secret of it was, as he has told me, his constant habit of asking advice, in everything, of God."

"Experience had declared too well his mind was built of water;
And so renouncing strength in self, he had fix'd his faith in God."

Towards the end of the year, the expedition—now at liberty from the pressure of the Indian crisis—prepared to storm Canton. The Emperor did not dare to make peace till the city had been taken; and Yeh, knowing that its surrender would be ruin to himself and his family, did not dare to give it up, determining "rather to blow the whole place into the air." There was, therefore, no alternative but to strike a decisive blow. Accordingly, at the end of November, the fleet was ordered up the Canton River; and Bate, in the Actæon, proceeded to join the force.

His last Sunday on shore was spent at Hong-Kong; and it almost seemed as if a presentiment had taken hold upon him that he should, ere long,

> "Speed, emancipate, to where the stars are suns."

"That day," writes a survivor who knew him intimately (the wife of Mr Parkes, the Consul), "he was with us, at a mutual friend's house, where we both were guests. He received the sacrament with us; and, on leaving church, he took hold of my hand, and said—'I wonder whether we shall ever receive the sacrament together again?' During our walk, that afternoon, he spoke much of the uncertainty of life, and remarked, that, in going to Canton, he felt he ought to remember this especially; 'but,' he added, emphatically and with a sweet smile, 'I know I am safe in the arms of my Saviour, in life or in death.'"

The presentiment shewed itself in another little incident. "When he was ordered up by the Admiral for service at Canton," writes the Colonial Chaplain, "he gave me his instructions and papers, to be kept in my iron-safe; adding, 'If anything should befall me, deliver these into the hands of the Admiral.'"

The day before he sailed, we have a glimpse of him, in his cabin, in the Actæon, at his favourite occupation—studying the Scriptures.

Havelock devoted two hours, every morning, even in his busiest days, to quiet meditation over the Word. "The walls and trees of my orchard, could they speak," said Bishop Ridley, "would bear witness, that there I learned by heart almost all the Epistles,—of which study I shall carry the sweet savour with me to heaven." Bate, too, loved his Bible; and many a quiet hour was given to its holy teachings.

That morning, there was breakfasting with him a friend who had come to bid him farewell. When breakfast was over, they took up the Scriptures, and read and prayed together. Peter's denial presented itself. "A noble character!" Bate observed; "and, perhaps, he never loved his Lord more intensely than when weeping over his denial of Him."

A little afterwards, they came upon Herod the tetrarch and the dark scene in the fourteenth of St Matthew. "Why," remarked Bate, "did Herod speak respecting Jesus to his *servants?* Was it, that Joanna, his steward's wife, had been healed by Him, and had followed Him and ministered to Him, and then that probably the 'servants' would thus know more about Him than any of the nobles of the land?" His friend now inquired if he had seen "Blunt's Undesigned Coincidences," adding, that this incident was mentioned in it as a striking example of "coincidence without a design," thus proving incidentally the truth of the Gospel-narrative. "No," said he, "I have never seen it, but these things interest me greatly."

A poet writes,—

"The Bible only stands neglected there,
Though that of all most worthy of his care;
And, like an infant troublesome awake,
Is left to sleep for peace and quiet sake."

Not thus did Bate treat the Word. "His perfect equanimity," writes a surviving friend, who knew him well (Captain Collinson, R.N., C.B.), "was the result of a continual study of the Holy Scriptures." When he fell at Canton mortally wounded, there was found in his pocket, all stained with blood, a little book of "Scripture-promises," with these two texts hastily marked, evidently that very morning—"We *know*, that, if our earthly house of this tabernacle were dissolved, we have a building of God, an house not made with hands, eternal in the heavens;" and, "*Through God* we shall do valiantly." "That field of promise," says the same poet,—

"How it flings abroad
Its odour o'er the Christian's thorny road!
The soul, reposing on assured relief,
Feels herself happy amidst all her grief,
Forgets her labour as she toils along,
Weeps tears of joy, and bursts into a song."

Few understood the secret; but not often has the light shining in the lively oracles transfigured a daily walk into a brighter "living epistle," than was seen in the brave officer whose brilliant apotheosis we are about to record. "His holy, consistent life," says a friend who parted with him for the last time that day before sailing for Hong-Kong, "contrasted so strongly with the world! His bright, joyous face, was such an index of his noble character! None could gaze upon it without seeing he enjoyed a peace which nothing could take away. And he was so fervent in spirit, serving the Lord."

A sailor of the Actæon, one day, not long after his captain's death, wiping away with his sleeve the tear from his weather-beaten cheek, said—"I never will forget the last sermon he preached to us. It was from the text, 'Not slothful in business, fervent in spirit, serving the Lord.'"

It was now to be seen, once more, how a Christian could deport himself in life's most trying crisis.

"I hear," wrote an old shipmate to him, that autumn, "that you are indispensable to the Admiral." Seymour knew what stuff he was made of; and he was not the man not to give him his right place.

On November 25, "On board H.M.S. Actæon, four miles from Canton," Bate writes to a friend in England, thus:—"We are now really mooring towards Canton. I came up here on Monday, and am now busily employed lightening the ship, to get her over a barrier which obstructs the passage about four miles below Canton. I believe I am to have the honour of leading the advance when we go up, as I know the river so well. I have had rather an anxious night: the junk alongside, with all our provisions and shot in her, sprang a leak, and we have been obliged to 'pump all night.' I see the gunboat for the mail is coming down, so I must close. God bless you!"

And again, thus:—"Those who have the conduct of affairs appear to think the *occupation* of the city the most serious and difficult part of the undertaking. Report says the Chinese are preparing all sorts of devilment, in the shape of pitfalls, mud-traps, &c. &c., and that they will not give up the city without a desperate 'stand.'"

Some days later, he addresses his old messmate, for the last time, thus:—"H.M.S. Actæon, off Macao Fort, Canton River, Dec. 4, 1857. My dear P——, On my return to Hong-Kong from the Straits of Banca, I found this ship. I have no heart for surveying; and I must seek the Lord for guidance and counsel to determine whether I shall remain after the Chinese affair is finished. I never forget my dear little godson in my prayers; but you know how feeble they are, and at times how distasteful they must be to an all-seeing God, who examines the heart to see whether the expression of the lips coincides. I have established morning prayers on board, which I pray may be accepted and blessed to the ship's company. I always do it after divisions, when the men are, as a matter of *mundane* duty, assembled. If I called them up specially for prayers, I don't think they would like it so well; besides which, the *officers* are on deck, and they are, as it were, *caught* by this arrangement. What think you? I like my officers very much. I must now tell you something about our doings on this river. The Plenipotentiaries of the four Powers are now at Macao, discussing, I believe, what we are to do with Canton. I think I told you that I had orders to consider my surveying instructions as subordinate to those I might receive from the Admiral for the conduct of the war. He has kept me on purpose for it; and I have now the honour to be the advanced ship in the expedition, being at anchor close off my old place, Macao Fort. We were to have made an advance last week; but as the last division of marines had not arrived, it was put a stop to by Lord Elgin. I had some difficulty in getting this ship (drawing 17 ft. 3 in.) over the barrier. We lightened her 15 inches, and took a night spring-tide to cross, the passage being lit up with red and white lights. She came over beautifully, just scraping the stones. I believe I am to have the honour of leading the advance. How I wish the war was over! and, although I push for Actæon to be in the front, and have managed as yet to keep her so, I am no lover of the work. People have a strange notion that Christianity and *work* are incompatible. My great desire is to prove this to be erroneous; and if God bless my labours, I look upon it as a mark of His approbation. I wish the world to see that the Christian officer is the best officer, ready for anything. It appears to me to be a principle little understood, though acknowledged in a general way, that religion arms the heart and steels it in the day of battle to meet all foes and to be dismayed at no dangers; for he who has Christ *feels* that for him to live *is* Christ—to die, gain; and whatever success attends him, is sanctified to him, and the glory of God is demonstrated.

"How glad I shall be," he continues, repeating once again a yearning of his gentle heart, which seemed to be deepening in intensity as it was on the eve of being dashed for ever from him, "to get quietly settled down in a nice little cottage, with a still nicer little wife. I don't expect ever to be an Admiral; and, if I am, I shall be *too* old to serve with advantage to my country. I had much better be rearing little ones to take my place. Do you not think so?"

And he adds:—"I think we shall be making an advance on Canton soon now,—perhaps next week. We are only waiting for the Plenipotentiary to say, 'Go.' Our dear old chief is beloved by every one. He *is* such a gentleman, and does things in such a quiet way. May the Lord bless us and prosper you in all your undertakings! Pray for me always; for I have much need of grace to walk a consistent life."

The same day he sends a message to his old friend's wife, thus:—"We are now very busy preparing for an attack on Canton. Actæon is at present the advanced ship, and, with our heavenly Father's will and blessing attending our feeble labours, will, I trust, keep so. I do hate and abhor war; but, as it is a necessary scourge, and one which God inflicts on us for wiser purposes than we can tell (for we see only 'through a glass darkly'), I like to shew the world that the Christian officer can be foremost in his country's cause; for surely, if our religion is anything, it ought to give us courage in the hour of danger. Have you read the Life of Hedley Vicars? What a noble man! After the perusal of it, it makes one feel frightfully humble. How short we come of *his* bright standard!"

And, on Dec. 8, also "On board the Actæon," he writes:—"I am commencing this, some time before the mail leaves; for I expect to be so very busy, in a few days, that I shall hardly have time to write. Our forces are nearly all out, the Adelaide having arrived with detachments. The Princess Charlotte, Blenheim, and Sans Pareil, are expected hourly; the French are all ready; and we are now only waiting for the Plenipotentiary to say, 'Go on.' They have had a grand conference at Macao. Of the result no one knows, except that it is agreed that the French take part. This I am rather sorry for: we ought to have taken Canton ourselves, and *then invited* France to go on with us. However, He who rules the destiny of nations directs also the counsels of the Plenipotentiaries: so, come what it will, it is of the Lord. He 'creates good' and He 'creates evil:' we see only 'through a glass darkly;' but the true light will be revealed to us hereafter."

Two days later, he continues:—"*Dec.* 10. I have just been inundated with a lot of Frenchmen—diplomatic and executive—who have come to the front to 'makes see figure.' To-morrow we go up to Canton in two gun-boats, with a flag of truce, to deliver the 'ultimatum;' and on Monday we advance, for the purpose of taking possession of part of the Island of Honan, and of mounting the wall by the south side of the city, pending Mr Yeh's reply. If he do not concede our demands in a given period (ten days), the combined forces of England and of France attack the city. The inhabitants have been warned to take such steps as they think advisable, under the circumstances, to save their lives and property.

"As the mail," he proceeds in the same letter, "does not leave this part of the river till Sunday afternoon, I have to give you an account of the proceedings which come off to-morrow. I don't think Yeh will yield. He cannot concede our demands without ruin to himself or family. The old fellow might get over the difficulty by eating gold-dust; perhaps he will do so. I have forwarded 'our allies,' with a copy of my surveys. The French officers dined with me yesterday; and I breakfasted with them to-day, after which I received a 'Memo' from the Admiral, nominating me as the officer to go to Canton (with the Chinese secretary) to deliver Lord Elgin's and the French minister's 'ultimatum.' This is an honour I confess I did not expect."

The day following he writes to Captain Collinson:—"Here we are, two miles in advance of all the squadron. To get here, I had to lighten the vessel fifteen inches, and, at the top of the highest night spring-tide, *scrape* her over the barrier. To-morrow we go up off Canton with a flag of truce to deliver Lord Elgin's and the

French minister's ultimatum, which, if old Yeh do not accept within ten days, we attack the city. I hope to get Actæon right off the place, and our dear old Admiral allows me to take her just where I think proper. On Monday we advance, and occupy all the approaches to Canton, the marines taking possession of that part of Honan facing the Factories, pending Mr Commissioner Yeh's reply. Gold-leaf now is his only recourse, if he wish to die *honourably*, as they call it." And he adds:—"What noble fellows we have in India! Talk of England's sons degenerating! Not while there is a Havelock or a Salkeld left. Those are the fellows who deserve victory."

And, three days later, he says:—"We went up off the city in two gun-boats, one French and one English, each towing a gig with the flag of truce flying. When near the appointed spot, a mandarin's boat met us, to which we pulled and delivered the 'ultimatum.' The poor fellow quivered like an aspen-leaf. I made a good reconnoissance of the place, and found they had made little or no preparations for defence,—at least on the river,—all the forts being in the same ruined state as when we left them, now nearly twelve months ago. The river is not even blocked up; and there is plenty of water for the Actæon to go up at high water. After delivering the letter, we returned to our advanced position off Macao Fort."

And he adds:—"We shall advance to *occupy only*, on Monday. Yesterday, my cabin was in a sad state of confusion: I had Mr Wade, the Chinese Secretary, staying with me; and my friend Parkes had just arrived; they were both busy interpreting, whilst the Chinese block-cutter was grinding away at the types in the fore-cabin. I send you a copy of the 'ultimatum,' which has been produced in my cabin: the English of it you will see in the 'Illustrated News,' and also a picture of Yeh and of his old father, which I allowed the 'Correspondent' to copy from those hanging up in my cabin. I am writing this in great haste. May God bless and preserve us all, and may He spare me to meet you before many more Christmas-days pass!"

An affecting postscript follows:—"I really do not think I can go on with this horrid surveying, after the war is over. Do, dear ones, *all* of you make it a subject of prayer, that I may be guided by Infinite Wisdom in the matter. I do not wish to give up my prospects in the service; but I find this incessant surveying such a terrible drag and tie to me! However, before I decide, I must let events develop themselves a little. 'Sufficient unto the day is the evil thereof.' Yours in much affection."

Yes, brother! thy future is arranged for thee by One whom thou wilt never have to regret that thou hast loved or served too well. Thou passest into the din of mortal strife with little before thee of this world's sunshine; but a better sun will ere long rise upon thee—a sun which shall never set.

"To go where God may lead thee,
To live for Christ alone,

To run thy race unburden'd,
  The goal thy Father's throne;
To view by faith the promise,
  While earthly hopes decay,
To serve the Lord with gladness,—
  Be this thy work to-day!"

CHAPTER XX.

"JESU is in my heart; His sacred name is deeply carved there."

"How I wish I could live to Christ! But—carrying about, as I do, this 'body of sin'—I can hardly realise that 'to die is gain,' although I know that 'to depart and to be with Christ is far better' than remaining here. We must, however, all wait, until the Lord has done with us." So wrote Bate, about the middle of December, as he was still moving up the Canton river, on his way to storm the city.

> He has communed with One whose converse sweet
> Has been of the Invisible and True; he expects
> Nought less than an *eternal* rest above.
> This hope it is which makes earth's sorrows 'light,'
> Which gives the 'weight' to glory yet unseen;
> This cheers him on his solitary road,
> When dearest ones have left him for the grave;
> This bids him smile at pain, and welcome death."

He learned that day of a friend's departure. "I am deeply grieved," he writes, "to hear of Colonel Lugard's death, although I believe he is far happier: but our loss is indeed a great one. May our heavenly Father be with each one of us, and preserve us from all danger!"

The crisis was now approaching. "We are now," he wrote, a day or two later, "only two and a half miles from the city. The *Highflier* is about three miles astern of me; my old friend is all right. The Admiral is expected hourly."

At last, on a dark, drizzling night—it was Saturday, the 19th of December—the *Actæon* anchored in the very centre of a vast mass of floating structures inhabited by an hundred thousand people. As the morning dawned, there was "a flutter and a panic among the dwellers on the water;" and the floating suburb, tier by tier, gradually melted away. Within three hundred yards of Yeh's yamun, the fleet lay moored in mid-stream, awaiting the expiry of the period of respite accorded by the Ambassador's proclamation.

Lining the shore, to the extent of half a mile, was a series of strongly-built brick "packhouses," each some two hundred feet in length, and one hundred in breadth, the roof thirty feet high, and supported by rows of square brick pillars. They were all open; and, before many hours, the largest of them was occupied by a battalion of marines. Beds of junk-matting were made up along the sides; arms and accoutrements were hung upon the walls and pillars; and in the centre-area the men were "squatting or lolling round their cooking fires, and frizzling their rations."

The owners, meanwhile, were clearing out from the

other warehouses their bales of cotton and their boxes of tea; for, up to the last moment, they had neglected the warning given them in the proclamation. A thousand coolies filled the narrow lane into which the doorways opened; and, protected by an English guard, the people were hastening away with their chattels, evidently feeling that the war was not with the population but only with their despotic governor.

A day or two afterwards, there was a reconnoissance, "to get a near view of the forts to the north of the city." The Admiral was there, and the General, and a large body of the allied force, with Captain Bate to map the country, and another officer to "take plans of the fortifications." "It was a beautiful breezy walk," says an eye-witness, "over a mile and a half of undulating country. We were now in front of the forts, which rise before us in extended panoramic view, stretching along a spur of the White Cloud mountain. Little parties of red-coats and blue-jackets were posted on different hills, to prevent our being cut off, and ready to support each other, whilst the reconnoitring party climbed the nearest elevations, where, within eighteen hundred yards of Gough's Fort, and within fifteen hundred yards of a heavily armed bastion, the chiefs took a survey through their glasses of the heights to be climbed. We are within range of all these guns, and tremendous in size they are. There are some fellows in that bastion, training a gun to bear upon us; and we expect, every moment, to see the puff of smoke. It was a rapid affair that reconnoissance. We returned as swiftly as we came, and were back in our quarters by six o'clock."

Two days later, another reconnoissance revealed the approaches of the eastern side of the city. At daylight the party struck inland over low hills covered with graves, and, crossing a paved causeway leading towards the town, hastened on over dry, hard fields of paddy, until they reached an eminence distant eight hundred yards from the east gate, and about as far from the eastern fort outside the city. The wall was hidden by intervening trees; but the fort was distinctly visible, and here was to be the route of the storming party at the assault. Over the wall was the northern half of the city, with no narrow streets, and containing the public offices and pleasure-grounds and the great yamuns. The fort had only to be taken "at a rush;" and from that position the wall must be breached or escaladed. The reconnoitring party were back to breakfast at eleven, having accomplished—chiefly through Bate's masterly dispositions—"a most satisfactory survey."

That afternoon, a fresh proclamation was issued, and distributed all along the Canton shore, announcing that Yeh had rejected the terms offered, and that, if the city were not surrendered within forty-eight hours, it would be bombarded and stormed. The people were warned to "clear out;" for the city *must* be taken and Yeh compelled to yield.

It was Saturday night; and the period of reprieve had expired without any symptom of submission. The

Sunday was observed as a day of rest, and one further opportunity given to the authorities to avert the impending catastrophe. "We open fire to-morrow at daybreak," Bate wrote, that day, to a relative in England; "and at noon I leave with the Admiral (being attached to his Staff), for the assault of the city the following morning. I have been *so* intensely occupied since we arrived off Canton, having the whole charge of placing the ships, and making plans for I don't know how many different departments. I never spent such a Christmas-day. I went to bed wearied in mind and in body."

Amidst the quiet, that evening, the brave man felt a fresh pang at the prospect of his future service. "Shall I," he wrote, "give up the Actæon or not, after this affair is over, *if* (the italics are Captain Bate's) I am spared to see it through? We must hold counsel of God. I wish very much to *serve;* but I am sick of this surveying. I have no energy for it now. Do, dear fellow, let me know your views. Perhaps I had better hold on, till I see my way clearer. As for working as I did in Palawan, I 'll not do it; it is of no use. I will do my work *conscientiously,* as unto *my* God and not unto man; and, if they are not satisfied, I don't care."

Ah! thy country should have spared thee, in this hour, that bitter pang.

"Generous and righteous is thy grief."

But,

"Count thou this for comfort—
Another world can compensate for all;

> The daily martyrdom of patience shall not be wanting of reward;
> Duty is a prickly shrub; but its flower will be happiness and glory."

It was his last Sabbath in this vale of tears, and it did not pass without leaving a blessing behind it. "I feel," were his words in a brief parting note to a friend that night, "that for me indeed 'to die is gain;' but I cannot say, 'To me to live is Christ,' for I feel how little I can do for Him. Yet I have that full trust in the finished work of the Saviour, that I have no doubts, no fears."

> "O day most calm, most bright!
> Thy torch doth shew the way."

Such literally was that day to him. Before another Sabbath dawned, he was to be with his Lord for ever.

A survivor of the ship's company remembers how earnestly he spoke to them that morning from the Scriptures, urging them most solemnly to lose not a moment in "fleeing from the wrath to come," and affectionately commending them to the grace and loving-kindness of the "Friend of sinners." Like Baxter of Kidderminster,

> "He 'd preach as a dying man to dying men;"

and such preaching is not soon forgotten.

A week or two previous, an officer was talking to a friend (the *Times'* "Special Correspondent") about him. "My pluck," said he, "is quite a different thing from Bate's. I go ahead, because I never think of danger. Bate is always ready for a desperate service, because he is always prepared for death."

"He'd learn'd to yield all praises unto Him who made him strong,
Who form'd him goodly armour, and who bore him through the strife,
Who cheer'd him on to victory with some guardian-angel's song,
Who gave to Faith the vision of the glorious crown of life."

A few days after that Sunday, another officer wrote:—"For coolness under fire no man ever excelled him, and few have been his equal. I see him now, standing on the ramparts at Macao Fort, with his broad chest fronting the rockets and gingalls discharged at us from the river-banks, as unconcerned as if God had placed a shield of adamant betwixt himself and the enemy. Ah! *I* have learnt a valuable lesson from him."

On the Saturday, a characteristic incident had occurred on board with one of his "mids." "That afternoon," writes the middy, "he looked at my accounts, as it was nearly the end of the quarter; and he said,—'I see I must let you have the money (£5, 4*s.*) which I lent you, till next quarter;' and when I said, 'Thank you, sir,' he said, 'Oh, I am not quite ruined yet; and I would sooner let you have a pound or two more than that you should draw an extra bill.' He then said,—'Now, you must pay everything; and as your next quarter's bill will be a heavy one, you can pay me then.'" The incident is trifling; but it indicates, not uncertainly, the generous heart of the man, and his wise, fatherly treatment of the youths under his command.

When Bate fell, the young mid wrote to his mother:—"Captain Bate's death, I am nearly sure, is the turning-point of my life."

It was no ordinary man whose daily walk thus told on a gay, thoughtless middy.

"Behold, what fire is in his eye, what fervour on his cheek!
Upon whose lips the mystic bee hath dropp'd the honey of persuasion,
Whose heart and tongue have been touch'd, as of old, by the live-coal from off the altar,
How wide the spreading of his peace!"

CHAPTER XXI.

"He look'd
Beyond the present to a distant world,
Where martyrs serve their God with ceaseless love."

It was a brilliant morning in the end of December (the 28th, 1857), and a city of a million of souls had scarce awoke from its slumbers, when "boom! boom! boom!" went our broadsides, and all Canton trembled.

On board the *Actæon*, that morning, Captain Bate wrote:—"We opened our fire at daybreak; and every now and then the guns make my pen jump again on the paper. You must excuse this very hurried and short letter. I am just going off with the Admiral for the landing-place, which is about two miles to the eastward of the city. We stop out all night, and advance early in the morning. God abundantly bless you! Ever yours."

Later in the day, at "10.30 A.M.," he hastily added:—"You will see more about this affair in the papers, than I can tell you now, I am so pressed for time. The bombardment is going on. City on fire in four places. Troops preparing to land."

Before landing, he secured a few moments' privacy —the last he was to enjoy. Sitting alone in his cabin, with the Bible open before him, he spoke with his Father in heaven. "I fear," he had just written, as he marked the wild, thoughtless excitement around him, "that our poor fellows are sadly forgetful of all God's benefits." It was remarked that he was himself unusually grave that morning. Death,

> "The stern and silent usher,
> Leading to the judgment for Eternity,"

was hovering too near, in those volleys of guns and rollings of musketry, not to awe into a deep thoughtfulness a spirit like his. And yet

> "The dread was drown'd in joy."

Calm and self-possessed, and as if craving in that hour the fellowship of a kindred spirit, he called to him one of his ship's company, and they read together the ninety-first Psalm. Then, hastily adding to the half-finished letter on his cabin-table the words, "Read the ninety-first Psalm *for our comfort*" (the italics are Captain Bate's), he sallied forth to the post of action.

How characteristic of the man—the reading of that Psalm! "Thou shalt not be afraid," it said, "for the terror by night, nor for the arrow that flieth by day." And again—"He shall cover thee with His feathers, and under His wings shalt thou trust." And yet again—"Because thou hast made the Lord, which is my refuge, even the Most High, thy habitation; there shall no evil befall thee." No, the promise of his

Father could not fail. It was "no evil" to remain in this vale of tears a little longer, if any work remained for him to do, or any grace to be brightened; and it was "no evil," to "depart," if already he were ripe for the glory.

> "'Twas joy to think thus far his race was run,
> So many toils and dangers safely o'er—
> His heart was fainting for his Father's land,
> His long-sought home seem'd nearer every hour."

And so he went out that day "comforted," to meet duty as became him.

At mid-day, he landed with the Admiral. The shells and round-shot were sweeping the wall of a fort (Gough Fort) on the heights; and Bate's party proceeded in another direction to reconnoitre. Before them lay a fort (Lin), which, as they approached, seemed to be deserted, when suddenly the lower embrasure was unmasked, and three heavy guns and a host of gingalls opened a galling fire. A village was at hand; and, under cover of its huts, the reconnoitring party, now supported by a body of artillery and of the 59th Regiment, brought the Enfield rifle to bear with such effect upon the Chinese gunners in the embrasures, that they could no longer stand to their guns. At length, some nine-pounder field-pieces were got into position; the place was battered and shelled; and, as a storming column were advancing to seize the fort, the "braves," after firing a parting volley, evacuated the embrasures and disappeared,—an English and French flag waving the next moment on the wall.

The afternoon was spent in desultory skirmishings on the neighbouring hills, preparatory to the grand assault of the morrow. Then came the night (says an eye-witness)—and such a night! The ships almost ceased firing; but the city soon became like a plain of fire. At first, it appeared as though the besiegers were bent upon reducing the city to ashes; but the destruction was not without a plan. There was a great blaze at the north-west angle, where was situated the Chinese guard-house, surmounting the gate. Shells and rockets were poured in volleys upon this structure; and it soon became a sheet of flame. By constant showers of rockets, the flame was led up and down the city-wall; and, in an incredibly short time, the long, thin line of fire shot high into the heavens, and then subsided into a smouldering smoke. The flames did not spread inwards, the object being to clear away, from the three spots marked out for the triple assault, a line of old houses which leant against the inner side of the wall, and afforded cover to those gingalls whence all our great losses, in affairs with the Chinese, have arisen.

Meanwhile, we have a glimpse of Bate in his last bivouac. "In the evening," writes his coxswain, who, with three more of his boat's crew, had accompanied him on shore, "I made the Captain's bed with straw, and the Admiral's, and mine, and the boat's crew's. I opened the Captain's knapsack, and gave him his night-clothes, and the Bible and Prayer-book; and he read prayers and a chapter in the Bible to me alongside of him; and then we had a little talk together, and he lay down, and so did I. The next morning I got up at three, and made some tea; and I had some, and my boat's crew. At half-past four, I roused the Captain, and he had a cup of tea. I opened his knapsack, and gave him his Bible and Prayer-book; and he read prayers to me, both kneeling. He got up and washed; and away he went with the Admiral. I packed up all our things, and put them on my back; and I and my boat's crew started after him,—the Captain, Admiral, and several other officers leading the way, and the blue-jackets and marines following."

As the day began to dawn, the rocket-practice gave place to a steady fire from a mortar-battery; and Bate's little party, now joined by the General and his staff, proceeded in the direction of the city-wall. The point of assault was some two hundred yards distant from the north-east gate; and they advanced, in the face of a running fire from the Chinese stationed all along the embrasures.

Arrived within about one hundred yards of the spot, they found themselves in a small village, having in front a huge tree, whose foliage hid it from the people on the wall. To the right, and separated from the village and the tree by a wide footway, was a little mud-built cottage, whose white-washed wall made it a conspicuous object in the morning sun. The cottage was entered by the Admiral and the General, accompanied by Bate and the other officers of their staffs. In a hasty reconnoitre, they found, some dozen yards

in advance, a ditch or gorge forty or fifty yards broad. In the intervening space was a low earthen fence, surmounted by bunches of high reeds, which interrupted the view of the spot where the scaling-ladders were to be placed to mount the broken embrasures. "All around," says an eye-witness (*Times'* Correspondent), "hurtled a storm of balls and rockets from the wall; and no one could cross to the edge of the ditch without imminent danger." Yet some one must run the gauntlet, if the ladders were to be set for the escalade.

One man, there, was always ready. He had been girding himself, that morning, for such a crisis as this; and it found him prompt to act. "Who can tell," he had more than once asked himself, since the little party left the bivouac,

"'The trials and temptations coming within the coming hour?'"

Suddenly a "trial" had come; and not a moment was to be lost in deciding. "Captain Bate," says the same eye-witness, "at once volunteered to go." As he rushed across the open patch, to look into the ditch, all eyes followed him, and more than one heart throbbed.

"He standeth a target-like Sebastian, and the arrows whistle near him;
Who knoweth when he may be hit? for great is the company of archers.
Every breath is burden'd with a bidding."

The "bidding" came. "Our Captain," says his coxswain, who was at his side, "was in the act of taking the distance from the ground to the top of the wall with his sextant, when a shot from a gingall struck him in the right breast. He fell straight on the ground, and never moved afterwards. I asked him several questions; but he could not speak."

In half an hour, he had ceased to breathe: his spirit had gone upward, to be with his dear Lord.

It was on the twenty-ninth day of December, and in his seven-and-thirtieth year.

"'No evil shall befall thee.'
Blest parting words!
I hear the echo of their music now;
Still he lives; for near Christ's burning throne
His spirit dwells, and tastes eternal joy:
Undaunted martyr-soldier!"

In the Roman catacombs, a monumental tablet was found bearing this epitaph,—"In Christ. In the time of the Emperor Adrian: Marius, a young officer; he had lived long enough; at length he rested in peace." Like him, our dear brother had "lived long enough." For this, it is not necessary to live to the season of gray hairs. A man may live long in a little time. Bate was taken in the heyday of nature's strength, "his eye not dimmed, nor his natural force abated;" but it was not too soon—no, it was not,—for he had won an unfading crown.

"Thou shalt watch no more, lingering, disappointed of thy hope:
Thy soul is alight with love,—glory, praise and immortality."

In Memoriam.

"The seed and dormant chrysalis bursting into energy and glory."

"I yearn for realms where fancy shall be fill'd, and the ecstacies of freedom shall be felt,
And the soul reign gloriously, risen to its royal destinies :
I look to recognise again, through the beautiful mask of their perfection,
The dear familiar faces I have somewhile loved on earth :
I long to talk with grateful tongue of storms and perils past,
And praise the mighty Pilot that hath steer'd us through the rapids."

"CANTON is taken," wrote a resident in China ; "but too high a price has been paid for it, in the fall of such a man as our dear Captain Bate."

"Our success," said the Admiral, in his official despatch, "has been damped by a great calamity, in the death of Captain William Thornton Bate. The sad event has thrown a gloom over the whole force."

"Men spoke of him," wrote one of his lieutenants, "with faltering tongues and swimming eyes. The loss was *felt*—felt by all, by men and officers, by the highest and the lowest."

"I was with him," wrote Mr Wade, the Chinese Secretary, "a minute before he was shot. Every one admits our success dearly purchased at such a cost. No man was more loved and appreciated, from the Admiral down."

"Captain Bate," said the *Hong-Kong Register*, "as usual, ever forward where duty called, was volunteering to place the scaling ladders when he was shot from the wall through the stomach. He died, as he had lived, a Christian hero, with the sounds of victory ringing in his ears."

"You people at home," wrote one of his mids, "cannot imagine (not even his sisters) how universally dear Captain Bate was loved and respected, from the Admiral down to the youngest boy in the fleet. This is without exaggeration; for I really never knew any man who enjoyed a more well-deserved affection and popularity. His officers and men have lost a kind friend and a patient adviser, who never tired of doing good, who entered into all their pleasures, and assisted them to the utmost of his power in all their difficulties. He was firmness itself, but so kind withal, that his most severe reproof was better received, and better attended to, than most men's praises.

> 'All felt his loss; his virtues we'd tried;
> And knew not how we loved him till he died.'"

We return for a moment to the fatal spot. "When I found the Captain was gone," says his coxswain, "the four of us carried him to a fort which we had taken, and laid him down. I remained by him till two in the afternoon, when a party of blue-jackets came from the city to carry him to the landing-place, and a body of marines to guard us. I and my boat's crew had to carry him over hills and valleys; we were all very tired; we got on board that night at eleven; we hoisted him, and then put him down in the cabin."

That noble countenance seemed to beam, even in death, with a certain heavenly halo. "Not a feature," says his lieutenant, "shewed sign or symptom of mortal agony; the calm, serene expression gave unerring indication of the peace within when his spirit, released from its trammels, had found rest from its labours in the presence of his God and Saviour. How striking a contrast this presented, when compared with those of the poor Chinese, on whose faces was depicted the intensity of malignant hatred, can only be remembered, not expressed or described."

At sunset, on the closing day of eighteen hundred and fifty-seven, his remains were committed to the grave in the cemetery at Hong-Kong. "Not a fold of his dress," writes an eye-witness, an officer of the fleet, "had been displaced. The doctor had placed him in his coffin in the dress in which he fell. Nor had any change at the last marred that peaceful expression which sat on his benign and benevolent countenance, whereon were stamped and sealed the virtues of his brave and manly soul. A retired spot in the grave-yard of the 'Happy Valley,' near Dr Gutzlaff and by the *ruins* of the little chapel, was selected by the Bishop, who performed the last offices for his friend."

The funeral is described by another officer of the fleet, thus :—" It was the most affecting sight I have ever seen. At three in the afternoon all the boats assembled near the Dove, and formed two lines ; and as there were several foreign men-of-war at Hong-Kong, and nearly all their officers and boats attended, they made two long lines. The afternoon was lovely, the magnificent bay like a polished mirror. All the ships in the harbour had their flags half-mast, and of course all the boats. The Tribune's barge had her band on board, and towed a cutter with the body, the coffin raised well above the gunwale, and the sailor's pall (the union-jack) drooping gracefully over coffin and boat : then another cutter, with the remains of the poor little 'mid.' As they left the Dove, the Tribune commenced firing minute-guns ; the barge and cutter passed down between the two lines of boats, pulling very slowly ; the band played the 'Dead March in Saul,' those glorious notes floating over the face of the waters not broken by a ripple, and the calm only disturbed every now and then by the roar of the minute-guns, which would reverberate and echo for a few seconds and remind one that the profession of him we mourned was that of arms ; and then again that exquisite music would swell, touching the very chords of the heart, and saying to us (at least to me), 'There is a heaven open for the Christian warrior ; he is passing from the din of war, from the turmoil of this life, to a new life, a new world, where there is no more death, no more war ;' and who could help feeling that this solemn scene was typical of what had taken place?"

And the same eye-witness adds:—"We formed in two lines after the boats with the bodies. All the marines and troops had fallen in, to receive and join the procession on shore. The pall-bearers were Major Casolet; Captain Dew, R.N.; Captain Bell, U.S. Navy; Captain Fabius, Dutch Navy; Captain Edgell, R.N.; Colonel Caine, Lieutenant-Governor: one hundred marines and soldiers, with one hundred blue-jackets, followed, and nearly the whole of the inhabitants of Hong-Kong."

"The scene," says another eye-witness, "was painful and mournful to a degree; and the not unmanly tear of sorrow fell unrestrainable from the eye of not a few of whom it might be said, 'Behold how they loved him!' The Governor, and his many friends, followed the chief mourners in the solemn procession; whilst the road was lined with other civilians, who stood with uncovered heads while passed the mortal remains of 'that heroic man, for whom all Hong-Kong mourns.'"

On the following Sunday, in St John's Cathedral, the Bishop gave vent to the grief which was weighing on so many hearts. "The loss which we have sustained," he said, "is the loss of no common man. Private intercourse of the most confidential kind, during an intimate acquaintance of more than twelve years, revealed to me in no common measure the excellent qualities of the friend in whose death, not only the service, but the whole foreign community in China, have experienced a heavy calamity. It is a blessed solace, amid the more than ordinary mourning caused by this melancholy event, to be privileged to cherish no doubt as to that state of glorious immortality into which our departed friend has entered. He fell in the service of his Queen and country. He has been taken earlier to his reward. He has received from the King of kings the highest promotion which a glorified spirit can receive. He is now singing the new song in the courts of paradise. He is now with that Saviour whom he long served on earth. He has departed and is with Christ, which is far better."

Six months afterwards, a friend in Hong-Kong wrote:—"I often visit his last resting-place—a quiet, peaceful spot, and there, recalling his words of tender counsel, pray that I may more closely follow in his footsteps."

About the same date, wrote another:—"His friends have made that quiet green mound a sweet spot, by surrounding it with the choicest and most delicate shrubs."

And another, in some simple lines, "dedicated to the ward-room officers of H.M.S. Actæon," embalms his fragrant memory thus:—

"Busy, O Death, thou art! thou and the Brave
Have form'd a fast alliance. Forth from our midst,
Daily some victim goes to thy embrace;
Whilst thou relentest not.
Yet one—ah! ONE—
Loved for his honour and his Christian heart,
The Hero, and the man—has gone to rest;

Pass'd through thy portals, Death, and smiled at thee,
For he fear'd not thy terrors.
Many a sailor on the pathless deep,
Whene'er he nears the coast of treacherous shoals,
Will bless the name and memory of him
Whose toil and science charted out their track.
Not on the couch where lingering sickness lies,
Not by decay of old and honour'd age,
He pass'd to glory;—but, in the duty-hour
Where England's chieftains are at all times found—
Beneath the battlement—before the foe—
There sigh'd he out a brave and glorious life."

A monument to his memory has since been erected on a conspicuous site adjoining the cathedral. "You can see it plainly," says a correspondent, writing on board H.M.S. Princess Charlotte, off Hong-Kong, of date November 30, 1861, "through one of the doors, as you sit in one of the front seats opposite the pulpit, —*and it is a sermon.*"

On the tablet at the grave in the cemetery is the following:—

"'The Christian parleys with no unmanly fears;
Where duty calls, he confidently steers;
Faces a thousand dangers at its call,
And, trusting to his God, surmounts them all.'

'When a man's ways please the Lord, He maketh even his enemies to be at peace with him.'

WILLIAM THORNTON BATE, R.N.,
FELL AT CANTON,
DECEMBER 29, 1857.
CAPTAIN H.M. SURVEYING VESSELS ACTÆON AND DOVE."

BALLANTYNE AND COMPANY PRINTERS, EDINBURGH.

JAMES NISBET AND CO.'S

RECENT PUBLICATIONS.

MEMORIALS of the REV. JOSEPH SORTAIN, B.A., of Trinity College, Dublin. By his WIDOW. Post 8vo, 7s. 6d. cloth.

"This is a charming biography. . . . The whole volume is replete with varied interest. We trust it will have a wide circulation."—*Record.*

THE LIFE and LETTERS of JOHN ANGELL JAMES, including an unfinished Autobiography. Edited by R. W. DALE, M.A., his Colleague and Successor. Post 8vo, 7s. 6d. cloth.

"Mr Dale has accomplished a difficult and delicate task with rare sagacity, fidelity, and success. . . . His criticism is reverent and discriminating. His biography is artistic and beautiful."—*Patriot.*

"The volume concludes with a chapter, by his son, on his home life, written with a truth, candour, and graphic skill, which give it a very honourable place amongst religious biographies."—*Saturday Review.*

LIFE-WORK: or, The Link and the Rivet. By L. N. R., Author of "The Book and its Story," and "The Missing Link." Crown 8vo, 3s. 6d. cloth.

"Every minister's wife should have a copy of this book, as the best guide she can have in doing good to the poor, and providing for the improvement of the neglected and the outcast, whom Christ came to seek and to save."—*Wesleyan Times.*

THE HARP of GOD; Twelve Letters on Liturgical Music. Its Import, History, Present State, and Reformation. By the Rev. EDWARD YOUNG, M.A., of Trinity College, Cambridge. Crown 8vo, 2s. 6d. cloth.

"Marked in an equal degree by unaffected piety and strong common sense; and for these and other reasons well worth perusing."—*Musical World.*

"We very earnestly commend this able and timely little work to our Episcopal friends, and to all who may have to do with Liturgical Music."—*Patriot.*

MEMOIR of the LIFE and BRIEF MINISTRY of the Rev. DAVID SANDEMAN, Missionary to China. By the Rev. ANDREW A. BONAR, Author of the "Memoir of Rev. R. M. M'Cheyne," &c. &c. Crown 8vo, 5s. cloth.

"The life of David Sandeman could hardly have been written by a hand, however unskilled, so that it should have been without interest, instruction, and reproof; but penned by the biographer of M'Cheyne, in his own genial, loving, and winning way, this memoir will be a permanent addition to our stock of religious biography. . . . . No reader can peruse this brief memoir without both pleasure and much profit."—*The Dial.*

SCENES of LIFE, Historical and Biographical, chiefly from Old Testament Times; or, Chapters for Solitary Hours, and for the Sunday at Home. By the Rev. JOHN BAILLIE, Author of "Memoirs of Hewitson." Crown 8vo, 5s. cloth.

"The topics of these meditations are generally well chosen, and the reflections founded upon them are such as they would naturally suggest to a pious and contemplative mind."—*Literary Churchman.*

ANNALS of the RESCUED. By the Author of "Haste to the Rescue; or, Work while it is Day." With a Preface by the Rev. C. E. L. WIGHTMAN. Crown 8vo, 3s. 6d. cloth.

"This is a deeply interesting volume. It is a book of similar character to 'English Hearts and English Hands,' and shews what may be effected by well-directed and individual efforts."—*Watchman.*

WORKMEN and THEIR DIFFICULTIES. By the Author of "Ragged Homes, and How to Mend Them." Crown 8vo, 3s. 6d. cloth. Also, a Cheap Edition, 1s. cloth limp.

"This is a book that we could wish to find extensively circulated among the working-classes. . . . The authoress has evidently studied her subject carefully, and she embodies in her book much valuable and pregnant information."—*Scottish Guardian.*

THE GRAPES of ESHCOL; or, Gleanings from the Land of Promise. By the Rev. J. R. MACDUFF, D.D. Crown 8vo, 3s. 6d. cloth.

"Mr Macduff has certainly produced a book of both pleasing and profitable reading."—*Witness.*

THE ROMANCE of NATURAL HISTORY. By P. H. GOSSE, F.R.S. With Illustrations by WOLF. Post 8vo, 7s. 6d. cloth.

"This is a charming book. . . This romance of natural history will be one of the best gift-books which can be procured for the season of Christmas and the New Year."—*Daily News.*

TRUE MANHOOD: Its Nature, Foundation, and Development. A Book for Young Men. By the Rev. W. LANDELS. Crown 8vo, 3s. 6d. cloth.

"This is a book true to its title . . . It is a book which every young man should attentively read, and every family possess."—*Northern Warder.*

EVENINGS with JOHN BUNYAN; or, The Dream Interpreted. By JAMES LARGE. Crown 8vo, 4s. 6d. cloth.

"The volume abounds in most valuable matter, eminently calculated to instruct and to edify. It is replete with interesting facts and circumstances, all in point, and appropriate citations from the Word of God, as well as from sacred poetry."—*British Standard.*

DAVID, KING of ISRAEL. The Divine Plan and Lessons of his Life. By the Rev. WILLIAM GARDEN BLAIKIE, A.M. Crown 8vo, 5s. cloth.

"The subject has been handled in a consistent and masterly way. . . . It is written with much clearness, eloquence, and force."—*Morning Post.*

BLACK DIAMONDS; or, The Gospel in a Colliery District. By H. H. B. With a Preface by the Rev. J. B. OWEN, M.A., Incumbent of St Jude's, Chelsea. Crown 8vo, 3s. 6d. cloth.

"This is a remarkably instructive and interesting book."—*Compass.*

"The object of the book is to depict mining life, habits, and character; this is done with great ability and success."—*British Standard.*

THE BLACK SHIP; and other Allegories and Parables. By the Author of "Tales and Sketches of Christian Life," &c. 16mo, 2s. 6d. cloth.

"This is an exquisitely beautiful little book. Its tales and parables are constructed with marvellous delicacy and skill—they are full of subtle and delicious fancy—they are rich in every line with deep and precious meanings. We give the book our warmest, most grateful praise; testifying that it has a spell over the minds of children more powerful than any book of the kind we know; and it leaves the most distinct intellectual and moral impressions on the mind. And it is intensely wise and religious, without a dull didactic word."—*Nonconformist.*

MEMOIRS of the LIFE of JAMES WILSON, Esq., F.R.S.E., M.W.S., of Woodville. By JAMES HAMILTON, D.D., F.L.S. Post 8vo, 7s. 6d. cloth.

"Dr Hamilton's book is one of the most satisfactory of its kind which it has been our fortune to meet with—one of those which most happily achieve the true end of biographical writing. We rise from the perusal of these memoirs with a conviction that James Wilson, whom we never saw, is as well known to us, *intus et in cute*, as if he had been one of our personal acquaintances."—*Spectator.*

THE OMNIPOTENCE of LOVING-KINDNESS: Being a Narrative of the Results of a Lady's Seven Months' Work among the Fallen in Glasgow. Crown 8vo, 3s. 6d. cloth.

"The title of this book almost claims for it a favourable notice. We are glad, however, to say that its pages, more than its title, deserve this at our hands."—*Scottish Press.*

HELEN DUNDAS; or, The Pastor's Wife. By ZAIDA. With a Preface by the Author of "Haste to the Rescue." Crown 8vo, 2s. 6d. cloth.

"This is an exceedingly pretty, well-written tale. Its object, much better achieved than that of many a more pretentious volume, is to exhibit the pastor's wife as a true 'helpmeet' to her husband."—*Dublin Christian Examiner.*

HELP HEAVENWARD: Words of Strength and Heart-cheer to Zion's Travellers. By the Rev. OCTAVIUS WINSLOW, D.D. 18mo, 2s. 6d. cloth.

"This pleasant little book reads like a prose poem. It is replete with sound, searching, practical remark, conveyed in the winning and affectionate spirit, and with the luxuriant richness of phraseology by which the author is characterised." —*Scottish Guardian.*

THE SONG of CHRIST'S FLOCK in the TWENTY-THIRD PSALM. By JOHN STOUGHTON, Author of "Lights of the World," "Spiritual Heroes," &c. Crown 8vo, 5s. cloth.

"Mr Stoughton's volume may be earnestly and warmly recommended. . . . Its chaste piety will make it deservedly acceptable to a large class of readers. Looked at with the purpose of the writer, we know of no recent volume of religious meditation which is likely to be more profitably read or pleasantly remembered. It is a cheerful and harmonious rendering of David's celebrated psalm." —*Daily News.*

THE PENITENT'S PRAYER. A Practical Exposition of the Fifty-first Psalm. By the Rev. THOMAS ALEXANDER, M.A., Chelsea. Crown 8vo, 3s. 6d. cloth.

"Mr Alexander gives us a literal translation of his own, very accurate, with an analysis and explanation, in which some pithy things are drawn from old divines. The body of the exposition follows, and the whole is wound up by a number of other metrical translations, making the book all that can be desired for the pleasure and profit of readers who unite taste with religious feeling or desire. Of the exposition itself we cannot speak too highly. It is soundly evangelical and deeply impressive. The style is peculiarly lucid and terse; every sentence contains a thought, and every line a sentence."—*The Patriot.*

THE LIFE of the REV. RICHARD KNILL, of St Petersburgh. With Selections from his Reminiscences, Journals, and Correspondence; and a Review of his Character by the late Rev. JOHN ANGELL JAMES. By CHARLES M. BIRRELL. With Portrait. Crown 8vo, 4s. 6d. cloth. Also, a Cheaper Edition, 2s. 6d. cloth limp.

"An excellent biography of an admirable man."—*Record.*

"Mr Knill was no ordinary man, and to write his biography was a duty due both to his character and to his services. Mr Birrell has discharged this work with fair ability and good judgment. . . . Mr James's Review is an elaborate, discriminating, and suggestive performance."—*Daily News.*

QUARLES' EMBLEMS. With entirely New Illustrations, drawn by CHARLES BENNETT, and Allegorical Borders, &c., by W. HARRY ROGERS. Crown 4to, handsomely bound, 21s.; morocco, 31s. 6d.

"Each artist has done his task well—the borders, which are Mr Rogers' share, are in almost all cases exquisitely fine and fanciful, and admirably drawn."—*Athenæum.*

EXPOSITIONS of the CARTOONS of RAPHAEL. By RICHARD HENRY SMITH, Jun. Illustrated by Photographs, printed by Messrs Negretti and Zambra. 8vo, 8s. 6d. cloth elegant.

"The handsome book now before us, containing a photograph of each of the cartoons, with Mr Smith's very thoughtful and tasteful comments upon them, will serve to perpetuate and to improve the salutary as well as gratifying impressions which a view of those grand paintings must create."—*Daily News.*

SERMONS on the PARABLES of SCRIPTURE, Addressed to a Village Congregation. By the Rev. ARTHUR ROBERTS, M.A., Rector of Woodrising, Author of "Village Sermons," &c. Crown 8vo, 5s. cloth.

"An excellent volume of sound, practical instruction, well adapted for family reading."—*British and Foreign Evangelical Review.*

SERMONS on the BOOK of JOB. By the late Rev. GEORGE WAGNER, Incumbent of St Stephen's Church, Brighton. Crown 8vo, 5s. cloth.

"There is no attempt at subtle logic, or rhetorical eloquence, or learned criticism; but there is what is better than either—a plain and forcible exhibition of scriptural truth brought home to human hearts."—*Evangelical Christendom.*

HOME LIGHT; or, The LIFE and LETTERS of MARIA CHOWNE, Wife of the Rev. William Marsh, D.D., of Beckenham. By her Son, the Rev. W. TILSON MARSH, M.A. of Oriel College, and Incumbent of St Leonard's-on-Sea. Crown 8vo, 5s. cloth.

"Her letters are the best reflections of her cultivated mind and loving heart, as well as of the genial piety which diffused its fragrant odour over all her works. We heartily recommend it to the notice of our readers."—*Record.*

A MEMOIR of the late ROBERT NESBIT, Missionary of the Free Church of Scotland, Bombay. By the Rev. J. MURRAY MITCHELL. Crown 8vo, 6s. cloth.

"The memoir of such a man as Robert Nesbit must be valuable to the Church, and we are glad that the task of publishing his remains was undertaken by a kindred spirit."—*Record.*

LIFE in the SPIRIT: A Memoir of the Rev. ALEXANDER ANDERSON, A.M. By the Rev. NORMAN L. WALKER. With Preface by Principal CUNNINGHAM, D.D. Crown 8vo, 3s. 6d. cloth.

"The peculiar and pre-eminent value of the biography is, that it exhibits in practical embodiment and working the theory of conversion which excludes, and that which embraces, the Atonement. . . . We have said enough, we think, to convey to our readers some conception of the value and importance of Mr Walker's work. We very earnestly commend it to them for perusal and study."—*The Witness.*

CHRIST and HIS CHURCH in the BOOK of PSALMS. By the Rev. ANDREW A. BONAR, Author of "Memoirs of M'Cheyne," "Commentary on Leviticus," &c. Demy 8vo, 10s. 6d. cloth.

"There is a soundness in the work, because the writer admits an historical and literal meaning, as adapted for general usefulness, while he responds to the voice of the church in all ages by admitting that the Holy Spirit intended to teach all ages by the Psalms. The work is a discreet, pious, and learned production, far above many similar attempts to illustrate these devout compositions."—*Clerical Journal.*

THE PUBLIC SPEAKER, and HOW to MAKE ONE.

By a CAMBRIDGE MAN. Crown 8vo, 2s. 6d. cloth.

"Preachers cannot fail to be benefited by a candid perusal of this treatise."—*Clerical Journal.*

"There are a great many very sensible hints in this little book, which young men may study with advantage."—*Church of England Magazine.*

AN EXPOSITION of the SECOND EPISTLE to the CORINTHIANS.

By CHARLES HODGE, D.D., Author of "A Commentary on the Epistle to the Romans." Post 8vo, 5s. cloth.

"We are inclined to prefer this volume to any other which we have seen from his pen. . . . . The verbal criticisms, though numerous, are brief and to the point, never wearisome, or pedantic, or needless. . . . . Dr Hodge has produced a volume of great interest and value."—*Baptist Magazine.*

THE UNSEEN. By WILLIAM LANDELS, Minister of Regent's Park Chapel.

Small crown 8vo, 3s. 6d. cloth.

"We have been much interested in this series of Discourses upon the Unseen, as an able and vigorous, a full and impressive, setting forth of the leading features of a department of Divine truth too much overlooked."—*British and Foreign Evangelical Review.*

THE PERSON and WORK of the HOLY SPIRIT:

Being Sermons recently Preached in London by Fifteen Clergymen of the Church of England. With Special Reference to a Revival of Religion in the Church of God. With a Preface by the Rev. EMILIUS BAYLEY. Small crown 8vo, 3s. 6d. cloth.

"We heartily thank their distinguished authors for their praiseworthy and, we trust, not unfruitful efforts, to promote the study of the Spirit's agency, and a sound, because a spiritual, revival of religion."—*Scottish Press.*

THE PRECIOUS THINGS of GOD. By OCTAVIUS WINSLOW, D.D.

Foolscap 8vo, 5s. cloth.

"This is a volume rich in experimental religion, and intended to be the companion, in his hours of devotion and meditative retirement, of the experienced and spiritual Christian. . . . It will doubtless be to many, what its pious author intended it to be, a book cheering solitude, soothing grief, and dispelling doubt, depression, and gloom."—*News of the Churches.*

REMARKABLE ANSWERS to PRAYER. By JOHN RICHARDSON PHILLIPS.

Small crown 8vo, 3s. 6d. cloth.

"This is a delightful work on a subject of vital interest to every Christian. Its narratives are of a striking and interesting character."—*Banner of Ulster.*

"We commend the entire volume to the perusal of our readers."—*Wesleyan Times.*

THE EVANGELISTS and the MISHNA; or, Illustrations

of the Four Gospels, Drawn from Jewish Traditions. By the Rev. THOMAS ROBINSON. Demy 8vo, 7s. 6d. cloth.

"We thank Mr Robinson for this valuable contribution."—*Clerical Journal.*

"We welcome the volume before us as indicating a return, on the part of modern commentators, to a more correct appreciation of the value of Jewish tradition in Scriptural exposition."—*Baptist Magazine.*

THE HIGHER CHRISTIAN LIFE. By Rev. W. E. BOARDMAN.

Edited, with a Preface, including Notices of the Revivals, by the Author of "Memorials of Captain Hedley Vicars," and "English Hearts and English Hands." Crown 8vo, 3s. 6d. cloth.

"There is a freshness and force in the work which pleases us much, and we think it is calculated to do much good among professing Christians. . . . . The Preface extends to more than forty pages, and contains a rapid sketch, interspersed with facts, of the gracious revival which is now spreading so auspiciously through the Churches."—*Evangelical Christendom.*

THE TITLES of JEHOVAH: A Series of Lectures Preached in Portman Chapel, Baker Street, during Lent 1858; to which are added, Six Lectures on the Christian Race, Preached during Lent 1857. By the Rev. J. W. REEVE, M.A. Small crown 8vo, 5s. cloth.

"We have seldom met with sermons that approach more nearly to our ideal of apostolic preaching than these. There is no question as to the author's foundation or superstructure."—*Record.*

THE THREE WAKINGS, with HYMNS and SONGS. By the Author of "The Voice of Christian Life in Song," "Tales and Sketches of Christian Life," &c. &c. Crown 8vo, 3s. 6d. cloth.

"All of these poems mark an author of considerable ability, while many of them are full of great beauty and feeling. Indeed, taken as a whole, the volume will bear comparison with the works of those who have acquired a high reputation in the world of poetic literature."—*St James's Chronicle.*

"A very delightful volume of poems is that entitled 'The Three Wakings.' The pulse of poetic beauty throbs among its pages."—*Critic.*

"It will interest and delight the cultivated reader."—*Evangelical Magazine.*

HYMNS of the CHURCH MILITANT. Compiled by the Author of "The Wide, Wide World," &c. 18mo, 6s. cloth antique.

"It contains about five hundred sacred songs, admirably chosen from the writers of almost every age and country. As a gift book to a Christian friend we can hardly imagine anything more appropriate than this."—*Baptist Magazine.*

THE GOSPEL according to MARK EXPLAINED. By JOSEPH ADDISON ALEXANDER, D.D., Princeton. Post 8vo, 7s. 6d.

"The work is minute and full, but characterised by compression of matter and conciseness of statement. . . . . A sound theologian and an accurate grammarian, he exhibits the advantages of the combination and well-balanced action of the exegetical and doctrinal tendencies, by which at once a check is put on critical trifling, and the tyranny of dogma is kept from overriding the canons of criticism."—*Witness.*

HYMNS of FAITH and HOPE. By HORATIUS BONAR, D.D. Fcap 8vo, 5s. cloth.

"There is great sweetness both of sentiment and of versification in many of these devotional hymns."—*Evangelical Christendom.*

"A volume of hymns which glow with poetry and piety combined. Many of them have found their way to many circles, and are greatly appreciated."—*London Monthly Review.*

THE LAND of the FORUM and the VATICAN; or, Thoughts and Sketches during an Easter Pilgrimage to Rome. By NEWMAN HALL, LL.B. Small crown 8vo, 6s. cloth.

"This book will be read with much interest by all, and will amply repay the time and trouble bestowed on it. The controversialist will find in it much to startle and amaze his practised eye, and will, moreover, receive hints not entirely useless in his special pursuits. We rise from its perusal with pleasure and profit."—*Witness.*

THE VOICE of CHRISTIAN LIFE in MANY LANDS and AGES; Sketches of Hymns and Hymn-Writers. By the Author of "Sketches of Christian Life," &c. Small crown 8vo, 5s. cloth antique.

"Hymnology is not an easy subject on which to write a popular book, yet the author has made the attempt and succeeded. Its plan is partly literary, partly historical, and partly biographical. The style is lively and picturesque, and free from all reproach of dulness. The hymns are well chosen, and translated with care and fidelity. The biographical sketches are clear and vivid, and shew considerable insight into individual character. We can heartily recommend this unpretending book to those who have an interest in its subject."—*Guardian.*

www.ingramcontent.com/pod-product-compliance
Lightning Source LLC
Chambersburg PA
CBHW020355030726
47496CB00007B/2148

* 9 7 8 3 3 3 7 0 7 5 8 9 7 *